Jan's Sanctuary Walk

Jan's Sanctuary Walk

Patricia M. Daniels

BLADENSBURG,
MD

Ian's Sanctuary Walk

Published by
Inscript Books
P.O. Box 611
Bladensburg, MD 20710-0611
www.dovechristianpublishers.com

ISBN: 9781732112599

Printed in the United States of America

To my husband, Jeff, and daughters, Rachel and Cathy, who lived this journey with me. Also to my writing friends, Heather, Judy, Louise, Gwen, Don, Barbara and Melanie. Thanks for the endless edits.

Chapter One

Jan Hendricks shook the rain off her umbrella and left it open on her office floor. A thunderstorm, typical for May in Tampa, Florida, had roared through that afternoon, and Jan was glad she'd remembered to bring the umbrella. She needed it to get from the car to the hospital on her rounds while visiting church members. Sitting down at her desk, she glanced at her watch. She had ten minutes to go over her weekly pastoral report before her 4:00 staff meeting. As she picked up the report, the church receptionist, Bonnie, paged her through the office intercom.

"Pastor Jan, the District Superintendent, Reverend Jim Dean, is on the phone for you."

Jan's heart skipped a beat. District Superintendents didn't call to just chat. Could this be the phone call she'd been waiting for… an appointment to her own church? Springtime in the United Methodist Church also provided the opportunity for pastors to move to another parish. Jan had been at The First United Methodist Church of Tampa as one of two associate pastors for five years, and she desperately wanted to pastor a church on her own. But women in the Florida Conference had only been ordained to the parish ministry since 1975, and now, nearly eight years later, only a few served as lead pastors. *Please God, let this be about my own church.* She picked up the intercom phone. "Thanks, Bonnie."

Jan took a deep breath and pressed the blinking light on her desk phone. "Hello, Jan speaking."

"Hi, Jan. Jim here. Glad I caught you."

"Um, yes, hi, Reverend Dean. How are you today?" Jan cupped the phone under her chin and wiped her sweaty, rain-soaked palms on her skirt.

"I'm fine, Jan. I'll get right to the point. I'm just back from our final clergy appointment- making session for this spring, and I have good news for you. The Bishop wants to appoint you to your own church."

Jan gasped and almost dropped the phone. *Oh, dear God, thank you, thank you.*

Jim chuckled. "I knew this would please you, Jan, and I'm excited for you. You ready for the details?"

"Absolutely." She took a deep breath and tried to calm her beating heart. "Where is it?"

"Well, it's not close. In fact, it's the farthest church north in the conference. It's First United Methodist Church of Baylorsville and is about forty-five miles northwest of Tallahassee."

Jan's heart did another flop. *Tallahassee.* It seemed a million miles from Tampa and was in the middle of nowhere. *But my own church.* She changed the phone to her other ear and continued listening.

"I'm coming your way tomorrow morning, and I would love to share more details with you. Can you meet me for breakfast at 8:30? And I'll need an answer by the end of the day. We need to get these appointments set."

Jan ran through her mental calendar for the next morning. She'd need to leave early enough to get Carrie, her eight-year-old, and Sarah, her five-year-old, to school and daycare. She had no early morning appointments, but if she had, they would have been postponed. This was the meeting of a lifetime.

"Sure, fine, Reverend Dean. I can do that. Ben can come, right?" Ben, her husband of ten years, would certainly be affected by this move.

"Of course, I expect him to come."

After planning where to meet, Jan hung up. She sat for a few minutes, stunned. She wanted the chance to pastor her own church, but worried about Ben and the girls. How would they handle such a long move? She drummed her fingers on her desk and called Ben. He'd be home from his teaching job at Tampa College and have the girls back from school. She checked her watch. Jan would be late for her staff meeting.

"Ben," she said when he picked up the phone. "Jim Dean just called. They've got a church for me…"

"What?" Ben interrupted her. "Wow, that's great. Where is it?"

"Well, we've got a big decision to make. It's not close." She paused for a few seconds. "It's in a little town called Baylorsville, northwest of Tallahassee."

Jan heard nothing but silence. "Ben?" Her voice cracked. "You still there?"

"Yeah, I'm here." Ben stammered. "Tallahassee, huh." Ben's voice rose higher. "Whoa, that's definitely not close."

"No, it's not, and we have to decide by tomorrow afternoon. Jim wants to meet with us tomorrow morning for breakfast at 8:30. Can you come?"

"You bet, and even if I couldn't, I'd still come."

"Look, I'm late for my staff meeting. I'll see you at 5:30, and we'll talk then, okay?"

"Sure. The church is in Baylorsville, right? I'll get the atlas and look it up. See you later."

Jan put the phone down. Ben had sounded shocked. They'd talked many times of the possibility of her being a lead pastor in a church, but they never dreamed it would be so far away. Moving over two hundred miles was a huge change for her family. Ben had encouraged her to take a position as lead pastor, but he loved being a humanities professor at Tampa College. It was a prestigious job, and he had worked hard getting it. Would he be okay moving to the middle of nowhere? Could he get another teaching job? How many colleges were in that area of Florida?

Her heart was still pounding, and her face burned. This information couldn't be shared with anyone until she talked it over with Ben, so she at least needed to look calm. Taking a deep breath, she gathered her notes and left her office for the staff meeting.

But my own church…

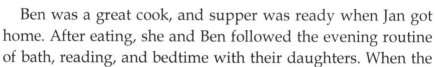

Ben was a great cook, and supper was ready when Jan got home. After eating, she and Ben followed the evening routine of bath, reading, and bedtime with their daughters. When the girls were asleep, they sat in the den to talk. Ben had the atlas open on the coffee table to North Florida.

"Here's the town." He pointed to a small, circled dot on the top part of the Florida panhandle close to the Georgia line. "It looks to be within an hour driving distance of Tallahassee and has a huge lake not too far from it."

Jan looked at the surrounding dark green around the tiny town of Baylorsville, which suggested miles and miles of undeveloped land, and her heart sank again. "It does look like it's in the middle of nowhere, doesn't it? And it's so far from here."

"Yep, that it is."

"Oh, Ben," her shoulders drooped, "we've never lived in a small town. How will we get by without the stores, the restaurants, the activities for the girls? And what about your job?"

"Yeah, I know. This isn't how I imagined our careers would flow. Always thought we'd be near a big city." He glanced at the stack of papers on the coffee table. Jan saw they were from his class. She immediately felt guilty. Ben had only been teaching three years at the college.

"I want my own church, Ben, but perhaps I should wait until a church opens closer to Tampa so you can still teach here." Jan stood and paced the small living room.

Ben grabbed her hand and pulled her to the couch. "Jan, we've been talking about the possibility of you getting your own church for a few years now. If you turn this down, it could hurt your career."

"I know," she interrupted him. "But what about *your* career? You want to stay teaching at the college level."

"Jan, I can always find a teaching position, even if it's in the local school system. And besides, you're ready for this." He put his arm around her. "You need to say yes."

Jan sighed and laid her head on his shoulder. Ben was her rock, had been since they met the second week of her sophomore year in high school in the coastal town of Clearwater, fifteen miles from Tampa. She thought him quite handsome with his dark brown, curly hair, wire-rim glasses, and a wide smile. From the first time she had mentioned being a pastor in their early days of college, he had supported her strong desire to become an ordained minister.

Jan blew out a long breath. "You're right. First Church Tampa is great, but I do want more. Preaching every Sunday, blessing and giving the Sacraments, being responsible for the church administration and programming, all sounds exciting. It's what I'm called to do. I'm ready for this challenge." She leaned back against the couch and stared up at the ceiling.

She sat up, almost knocking Ben in the face. "What about my parents? They've been so helpful with the girls." Jan's parents, Bill and Helen Sparks, still lived in Clearwater. Carrie and Sarah were their only grandchildren, and her parents doted on them. "They'll miss so much of our children's lives if they're… what?" Jan looked at the map again. "…five hours from them."

Ben tipped her chin up so she was looking at him. "Jan, I really think you should take this church." He smiled at her. "Your parents are retired and can come visit anytime. You need this."

Jan sighed again and pulled away from him. Ben was right. She wanted this church. Few churches were willing to have women as lead pastors, and if she turned this down, it might be years before she got another opportunity. A knot formed in her stomach. Not only did she worry about her family, but she also worried about herself. Pressure from conference officials and clergy, especially clergymen, demanded clergywomen do well as lead pastors. She could not fail.

"But the girls?" She got up and paced again. "Will they be okay? And the schools? Is the Baylorsville elementary school even accredited?" Jan ran her hands through her hair, causing it to stand up.

Ben pulled her back on the couch and smoothed her hair. "I'm sure the school will be fine. You remember what we promised each other when you got ordained." She leaned against him, knowing what he would say. "We'd be open to what God was leading us to do." He lifted her chin up so she was looking into his eyes. "We wouldn't be afraid of change."

He pecked her on the cheek. "This is an incredible opportunity for you, and, who knows, maybe me, too." He laughed. "And it's not like we'll be there for years. Remember, the United Methodist Church moves its pastors around every few years."

Jan nodded. "Yeah, you're right. We agreed to move forward toward change, not away from it. But this church is a long way from our support system. It would be easier if we weren't so far away from everything."

Ben laughed again. "You're acting as if Baylorsville is on another planet. It might be in the middle of nowhere, but Tallahassee's a big town. And I checked the schools. There are at least three colleges there: Florida State University, Florida Agricultural and Mechanical University, and a smaller, newer community college. I'm almost at the end of my semester here. I can put together a resume and send it to those colleges before we even move." He got up and pulled her up with him. "Let's pray and get to bed. Tomorrow will be an emotional day."

Jan nodded, and they both headed toward the bedroom. Her mind was still racing with questions.

The next morning, Jan and Ben met Jim at a small restaurant near the church. Jan had tossed and turned all night, debating the pros and cons. She finally slept, after realizing she needed more information to make this decision.

They joined Jim at a corner table.

"You two ready for this?" Jim asked. He was going bald, with a few tufts of silver hair around the bottom of his head. Jan liked Jim. He had supported her from the day she was appointed to First Church Tampa. She knew he had gone to bat again for her to get this church.

After they ordered their food, Jim brought out a sheet of paper and handed it to Jan. It held the details of the church. Jan's hands shook as she and Ben read the information.

While they read, Jim chatted about the church. "It's healthy, with a membership of three hundred, averaging about half of that in worship each Sunday. There's a good mix of families and older folk." He went on listing the statistics of the church as Jan's hand clutched Ben's under the table, and her heart pounded. *This sounds wonderful, but….* The questions whirled through her head.

Jan waited until the waitress had placed their food in front of them, a full breakfast of scrambled eggs, bacon, and toast for Jim and Ben, and a single English muffin for her. "I have lots of questions, but perhaps the most important one is, will they accept a woman?" She looked at Jim, trying to read his face.

He just smiled at her. "Yes, Jan, they'll accept a woman, especially you. I've already talked to the staff parish committee, and they're excited you're coming."

Ben slapped the table with his left hand and put his right arm around Jan. "I told you, Jan. I know you'll do great."

She took a deep breath, squeezed Ben's hand, and, her voice shaking, said, "We'll take it."

For the next six weeks, Jan and her family encountered a whirlwind of meetings, goodbye parties, packing, and praying. By the middle of June, they were on their way to an entirely different world.

Chapter Two

As the exit sign for Baylorsville, Florida, came into view, Jan's heart fluttered. She tucked her hair behind an ear.

"Here we go," she said to her mother, Helen, who had accompanied her on the long car ride from Tampa. She glanced in her rearview mirror over the heads of her two daughters to where Ben was following her in a five-year-old red Ford Mustang. Her dad, Bill, trailed Ben in a thirty-foot U-Haul, which carried all their possessions. Sighing, Jan turned on her blinker and slowed down for the exit.

Helen reached over and put her hand on Jan's arm. "You'll do great, Jan. God has been preparing you for this for a long time."

Jan glanced at her mom. "I know, Mom. But everything's so different. And I'm worried about Ben and the girls. I hope they'll be okay in this small town." More so, she was afraid she'd forget the skills she had learned and make a mess of leading this church as their pastor.

She concentrated on driving her station wagon down the long, tree-lined exit. "What if the people don't like me, or stop coming because of me? They've never had a woman pastor before. And I'm preaching every Sunday. I like to preach, but I've never done it every Sunday." Jan had only preached once every three months at the Tampa church. *Will I even have enough to say?*

When Helen didn't speak, Jan glanced at her. Her mom had that "don't give me excuses" look she had used every time Jan complained as a child that something was too hard.

Jan laughed. "Okay, I know I'm whining."

"Yes, you are."

"And you don't need to remind me I asked for my own church. I am ready for it, and even Ben is excited for me."

"Yes, you are. You did an incredible job in Tampa. This church is lucky to have you."

Jan laughed again. "Well, you're a little biased, but that's okay. I appreciate your support."

Helen smiled and sat back against the seat.

Coming to the end of the exit road, Jan turned right onto the two-lane road lined with thirty-foot pine trees. She rolled down her window just enough to lift her hand in a wave to her husband. He blinked his lights in response. *Please let Ben find a teaching job.* He so loved teaching. And it would be tough for them with only one income.

Jan heard a soft sigh from the back seat and glanced into the rearview mirror again. Her daughter, Sarah, was awake.

"Are we there yet? Are we there yet?"

Sarah's honey-colored hair was mussed, and her cheeks flushed with sleep. Jan could see Sarah twisting in her seat belt, trying to take in all the sights, and her daughter's excitement warmed Jan's heart.

Jan gave a quick glance toward her second born. "We're almost there, Sarah. Make sure you stay in that belt."

"Okay," Sarah said, straightening in her seat.

Carrie, Jan's older daughter, spoke up. "Wow, these trees are huge." Jan's eyes flicked quickly to Carrie, who had put her book down and had pushed her light blue glasses up to look out the window.

Jan turned back to focus on her driving. "Yeah, the trees are much bigger up here in North Florida. There're even steep hills here. It's almost like we're in the mountains."

"And the ground's red!" Carrie exclaimed as the trees thinned out and red, clay dirt appeared on the side of the road.

Helen turned in her seat and laughed at Carrie. "It sure is, honey. Don't see any white sandy beaches like we have."

Helen was laughing now, but Jan knew her mother wasn't happy her granddaughters were moving five hours away. In fact, Jan knew her mother wasn't happy any of them were moving that far. A wave of sadness passed over her. This move was hard on everyone. *Was this right?*

Everyone quieted, and the small caravan began the final leg of the trip. Baylorsville was about twenty miles from Interstate 10. As Jan watched the huge trees reflecting through her windshield, she rewound the journey she had taken to get to this point in her life. Throughout her childhood and teen years, she'd been heavily involved with the church. Then, after entering college, she felt the strong call to become a pastor, which was unusual for a woman during the late 1970s. Her parents, and especially Ben, supported that call, and after graduation, she ended up in Seminary at Duke University. Four years later, she was ordained into the United Methodist Church, and then appointed to the staff at First Church, Tampa. She loved doing ministry within the context of a large staff, but she wanted more. She wanted to be the pastor in charge. Now she had that chance. And she had to succeed.

Reaching the town, her stomach began to roll. She rubbed it. *Hope I don't get sick.* She took a deep breath and willed her tummy to behave. Jan recognized some buildings. She and Ben had made a brief courtesy visit a month ago to see the church and parsonage, the home they would live in, and meet a few key leaders. They passed the local grocery store, the Dollar General, Posie's Flower Shop, and the Baylorsville Bank. They came to the top of a hill and the entire downtown of Baylorsville, only two blocks long, came into view.

"Wow," Carrie shouted, "the streets are brick!"

"Yeah, Mom, look," Sarah piped in.

Jan felt a blast of hot air come through the car. Carrie had rolled down her window and was almost hanging out of it. Sarah was squirming out of her seatbelt.

"Carrie, Sarah, both of you sit back in your seats," Jan called. "Yes, the street has bricks."

Jan steered the car off Main Street onto Call Street and the steeple of First Church came into view. As they passed the church, she saw the sign out front saying: *First United Methodist Church - Welcome Pastor Jan Hendricks and family.* She heard a honk behind her followed by an even louder honk and smiled. The men in her life were heralding her.

"Why did Daddy honk his horn?" Sarah asked.

"Look at the sign in front of the church, Carrie," Helen said, as she pointed.

Carrie beamed, "Oh, that's neat, Mom."

"What's it say?" Sarah asked.

Helen read the sign and both girls clapped their hands.

Jan's face flushed with pride. *Well, God, this is in your hands.* The fluttering in her stomach had eased, but now her heart raced. She hoped it was more excitement than fear.

"What a pretty little lake," Helen said, bringing Jan's thoughts back to the car ride. "I bet you'll be walking there often."

"I sure will," Jan said, glancing at the small lake on her mother's side of the car. "Looks like a lot of the town folk walk it." She saw two elderly people walking, even in the middle of the 90-degree June day. There were picnic tables on one side with a swing, jungle gym, and sandbox. Huge oak and pine trees towered over the other side. Jan sighed as warmth ran through her. Praying while walking had always been her saving grace when things got tough. Yes, this tiny lake would be her sanctuary.

The parsonage came into view. Jan and Ben had seen it on their earlier visit, but the girls were seeing it for the first time. Jan passed three cars parked in front. *Oh, no, people are already here.* She had hoped to have time to freshen up before meeting anyone. She pulled into the carport, while Ben parked beside her and jumped out to help Bill with the U-Haul. Jan peered around her mom at the cars.

"Looks like the welcoming committee is here," Helen said.

"Yeah, I called Betty Smith, the church secretary, when we stopped for gas and she said she would make sure people were here to help us unload," Jan said, as she climbed out of the car.

"Is this where we'll live?" Carrie asked.

"Wow," Sarah exclaimed.

The long, ranch-style brick house had four bedrooms, a study, a separate den with a fireplace, and a formal living room. The girls were thrilled they were going to have their own rooms. Ben had claimed the study, as Jan had one at the church. As Jan helped the girls out of the cart, her heart beat faster. Several people were waiting for them. She recognized Betty, and Nancy White, the chair of the Staff Parish committee. Jan smiled when she saw the two women as they had welcomed her warmly on her visit last month. *At least two allies.*

As Helen stepped out of the passenger side of the car, a middle-aged woman, who had been standing alongside the driveway, came up to Helen.

"Pastor Jan," she said, grabbing Helen's hand, "we're so glad you're here."

Helen laughed. "Oh, I'm not Jan, I'm her mother. This is Jan," she said, pushing Jan forward.

The woman's eyes opened wide and her face paled as she glanced at Jan. Jan's stomach dropped. Already people were thinking she didn't fit the description of a pastor. At thirty-three years old, and five feet, two inches tall, Jan still had a girlish figure and didn't look her age. Swallowing her nervousness and trying to maintain some confidence, Jan walked up to the woman.

"Hi, I'm Pastor Jan." She shoved her hand toward the woman whose face had now turned red.

"Uh, sorry ... Pastor Jan." The woman looked around as if trying to find someone to save her. "My name is Wilma Adams and I'm on the parsonage committee." She grabbed Jan's hand, pumping it up and down.

Jan breathed deeply and put on what she called her 'pastor's face,' which she hoped made her look alert, compassionate, and somewhat intelligent. "It's okay, Wilma. My mom and I have always been told we look alike. It's nice to meet you."

For the next ten minutes, as others came up to her, Jan introduced Ben, the girls, and her parents. Her ministry had begun. *God be with me.*

Chapter *Three*

"Where is it? I know it's somewhere here," Jan shouted. She flung an assortment of packing paper, cardboard boxes, and books around on the kitchen table.

"What're you looking for?" Ben asked, coming from the den where he had been unpacking boxes of books.

"My hymnal," Jan cried. "I need it for tomorrow. I've got to find it." She pushed the items around on the table, knocking paper on the floor. Perspiration ran down her face. She swatted at the drops on her forehead.

Ben picked up the paper and put his hand on her shoulder, which she pushed away. "Calm down, Jan. It's over there." He pointed to the kitchen counter where the hymnal lay by the phone.

"Oh, thanks," she grumbled. "Forgot I put it there so it wouldn't get lost in this chaos."

It was Saturday, three days after their arrival in Baylorsville. Bill and Helen had stayed to help unpack, but they'd only managed to do the bedrooms and the kitchen. They had left early that morning for the drive back to Tampa. Jan sighed as she picked up the hymnal. "There's still so much to do," she said, glancing at the dozen unopened boxes in the den. "And I must go to the church this afternoon and practice my sermon." She rolled her shoulders, hearing a snap.

Ben guided her to a kitchen chair and pushed the remaining

paper on the table out of the way. "Let's take a break. I'll get some iced tea and we can sit for a minute." He looked at the cabinets. "Hmm, where'd we put the glasses?" He glanced at Jan and grinned.

Jan chuckled. "They're in the cabinet over the sink." She watched Ben put ice in the glasses and fill each to the top. "Guess I'm a bit touchy," she said. Ben brought the glasses to the table, and she drank deeply.

"Well, it's hot and we're both a bit stressed." He gulped his tea.

Jan rolled her tight shoulders. "I want most of the unpacking done before I preach tomorrow. I have to feel settled."

Ben got up and took over massaging her shoulders. "I know you need to have your nest all ready before you start work, but the unpacking will get done."

"I just want it to feel like home." Because United Methodist parsonages came fully furnished, Jan had no say in any of the furniture. So, knick-knacks and pictures helped to make it their home. Ben collected civil war paintings his dad had given him. Those pictures would end up in Ben's study. And Jan had several framed pictures of both Carrie and Sarah. They captured moments of the girls from their birth to the present. She wanted those pictures to line the long hallway connecting the bedrooms.

Ben squatted beside her, tipping her chin up and kissing her on the cheek. "Jan, remember, I'm not working. I have time to get things the way we want them."

Jan flinched and pulled away from him. "Don't remind me you gave up your job to come here." She looked into Ben's eyes and immediately regretted her words. "I'm sorry, I didn't mean to say that." *I've got to calm down.*

Ben shook his head. "We've talked about my job many times. I'll find one. And if I can't teach in a college, I'll substitute in the school here. I truly believe God's got this. We'll be alright."

Before Jan could reply, Carrie and Sarah trooped into the kitchen. They had been playing in Carrie's room.

"Mom, we're bored," Carrie whined. She flopped on the

floor beside the table.

"Yeah, Mom, we miss our friends," Sarah echoed as she snuggled into the crook of Jan's arm.

Jan glanced at Ben and frowned as he shrugged. Not only was Jan anxious to get the house in order, but she was also concerned about the girls' adjustment to this new place. But just as she got up to help the girls find something to do, they heard children's voices outside. They looked out the back window and saw two little girls, blond braids dangling down their backs, standing in the backyard. As a gift to Carrie and Sarah, one of the men in the church had attached a tire swing to a huge live oak. The two girls were looking at the swing.

"Hey, that's our swing," Carrie said, heading to the back door.

"Carrie, those girls look to be about your age," Ben said, taking Sarah's hand and opening the door. "Let's go meet them."

Carrie bounded out the door and climbed on the swing. She eyed the older girl. Ben, with Sarah cowering behind him, approached the new girls. Jan followed.

"Hi, girls," Ben said. "We just moved here." He pulled Sarah from behind him. "This is Sarah, and that's Carrie." He pointed to Carrie, who had started swinging.

"How old are you girls? I bet you're the same ages as these two," Jan said, kneeling beside Sarah.

"I'm eight and my sister's five. She's going to kindergarten this year and I'm going into the third grade," the older of the girls said with her eyes still on Carrie and the swing.

"I'm going into the third grade, too," Carrie said. She was now twirling in the swing. "Do you want to swing?"

The older girl grinned. "Sure, my name's Wanda, and that's Mary. We live over there." She pointed to a house two doors from the parsonage.

Carrie jumped off the swing and Wanda climbed on. The girls immediately began chatting.

Sarah and Mary sat on the ground and began talking, too.

Jan looked at Ben and smiled as they walked back to the

house. "At least the kids have met friends. How amazing they're the same age." She was glad the girls had provided an interruption to her little outburst.

"Yep. Perhaps that's a God thing." Ben put his arm around her as they entered the house. "By the way, how's the sermon coming?"

"It's done," Jan said. "But I want to preach it out loud this afternoon at the church, get the feel for it. I also want to test the microphone. I sure hope the sound system is okay. I've already heard rumors people expect they won't be able to hear me."

"Why's that?" Ben asked, wrinkling his brow.

"Because I'm a woman." Jan vividly remembered the first time she spoke in her previous church. Even though the church had held over seven hundred people and had a great sound system, people still said they couldn't hear her. And to Jan, that translated to women shouldn't be preaching. She feared the people of Baylorsville would react the same way.

"Well, that's silly. You're a great preacher, and the church isn't that big. I'm sure they'll hear you. Besides, you'll win them over right away."

"Thanks." She hoped he was right.

"You can do this, you know," he said.

Tears sprang to Jan's eyes. At least Ben believed in her. She just had to believe in herself.

"Why don't you go to the church now and test the sermon. I'll unpack more boxes and have lunch ready when you get back. Perhaps we can put the pictures up this afternoon and then rest."

Jan pecked him on the cheek. "You're the best." She gathered her Bible, hymnal, sermon notes, the bulletin and left.

Even though it was hot, she walked the half-mile to the church. But as she passed the small lake, she stopped. A mulched walkway surrounded it. On impulse, she turned onto the path. The smell of fresh-cut grass and wet dirt lifted her spirits. A mockingbird started its repertoire.

Oh God, she prayed silently as she walked, *be with me. Let me be who you need me to be in this church. Keep me open to your will. Help me be the conduit of your love. Help me remember that you are in this. You know how scared I am. Yet I can't let it show. But, it's not even me doing this. You're doing this. So, give me the skills I need. Put people in my path who'll help me run this church.*

As she walked, her anxiety lessened. Ben was fully capable of unpacking and getting the house in order. And their daughters were already making friends. Jan needed to relax and concentrate on her job.

Be with us, God. Help us become a part of this town, and most of all, help us enjoy this journey. Amen.

She stopped and realized she had walked around the lake three times. Yes, this lake would become her sanctuary. Feeling more confident, she continued her walk to the church.

This would be the first time she was in the church by herself, and Jan wanted to soak it in. The red bricks and high steeple were typical of the churches in the Deep South. She was told it had been built in the 1950s. The twelve steps leading up into the sanctuary were wide and made of concrete. Jan cringed as she realized older folks probably had trouble getting into the building. A wing to the right held Sunday school classes, and a new fellowship hall in back held the church offices. Holding to the custom of small-town churches, the sanctuary was not locked, so she opened the door and went in. The smells of old candle wax, musty rugs and the lingering odor of perfume immediately enveloped her. *I love the smells of a sanctuary.* It was also hot. The air conditioner would not be turned on until early Sunday morning, so she hoped she could test the microphone and read through her sermon quickly.

She walked down the middle of the church. The deep red carpet, covering the center aisle and chancel area stood in stark contrast to the rich, polished browns of the pews. An altar rail cordoned off the raised chancel, which held the central pulpit with the choir loft behind. It surprised Jan to see the pipes running up the wall behind the small organ. She hadn't known the church had a pipe organ. It stood on one side of the chancel with a black grand piano on the other side. She stepped into the pulpit, looked out over the empty pews, and imagined them full.

"God's love is everlasting…" She started practicing her sermon.

Chapter *Four*

Jan rose at six a.m., her first Sunday. It was an hour before she normally got up, but she wanted to go over her sermon once more before facing a sea of unfamiliar faces. This first Sunday needed to go well.

She took a quick shower and blow-dried her hair. Adrenalin pumped through her body making every action sharp and focused. She applied eyeliner and mascara and stepped out of the bathroom to get dressed.

"Sleep okay?" Ben asked, rolling out of bed.

"Yeah, surprisingly well."

"Ready?"

"I think so," she said, giving him a quick peck on the cheek. She pulled on her favorite blue dress, which brought out the color of her eyes.

"You'll do great," he said, throwing her a kiss and padding into the bathroom.

I sure hope so. Jan walked to the kitchen, put the teapot on, made toast, and sat at the table. The rehearsal of her sermon had gone well yesterday. The microphone seemed to work okay. Being both emotionally and spiritually prepared boosted her confidence. Now she just needed to conduct this first worship service well. The people she had met while moving in seemed friendly and welcoming. But this morning she would meet the entire congregation. Her heart fluttered thinking about preaching in front of them. She remembered Reverend Dean saying the church had three hundred members, but only half of those were active. The pastoral support for the nine hundred attendees at her old church was shared by the staff, but now she was solely responsible for this congregation. *Be with me, God.* She sat at the table and reviewed her sermon one last time.

The service was going better than expected. The organist, Helen Hill, was incredible, and the choir sang one of her favorite anthems, "All is Well." Several times during her sermon, Jan made eye contact with members of the congregation. Smiles, nods, and even a few "amens" met her gaze. The people, her people, were engaged. As she neared the end of her sermon, her spirits soared.

"Our faith story is an important part of who we are," Jan said, finishing her sermon. As her gaze swept over the church once again, she noticed one man glaring at her. He sat next to a small woman. Jan paused, puzzled at his response, then shook it off and continued. "But so are our everyday stories. During the next few months, I want to get to know you and your stories." Jan took a pad of paper and stepped from the pulpit.

She held the pad up. "I'd like to connect with each of you. I could come to your house or meet you for lunch or dinner. This pad will be in the narthex, and it lists dates and times I am free. Please choose a time and write your name down. I look forward to getting to know you better."

She raised her hands. "Now let's stand and sing one of my favorite hymns, 'Amazing Grace.'"

She smiled as she caught Ben's eye, and he gave her a thumbs up. After the benediction, Ben and the girls joined her in the narthex, the lobby at the front of the sanctuary.

"Mom, look, it's Wanda," Carrie said as a small, pig-tailed girl ran toward them. The girls met and danced into a hug. Jan recognized her as one of the little girls in the backyard yesterday. A slight woman with a long blond braid down her back followed Wanda with little Mary trailing behind her. The woman grabbed Jan's outstretched hand.

"Pastor Jan, we're so glad you're here. I'm Linda Williams. I see our girls have already met." She glanced at Carrie and Wanda, then pushed a short, stocky man, with a ruddy complexion and deep blue eyes, toward Jan. "And this is my husband, Tom. We live two doors down from you."

As Jan shook their hands, Sarah pulled at Jan's robe. "Mom, can I go play with Mary?" Jan bent down and whispered into Sarah's ear. "Sarah, remember what I told you. No interrupting or calling me Mom until I get my robe off."

She had established that rule at her other church. It helped define her role with the girls. She didn't want to brush them off but needed to set a boundary while she was at church. Sarah stopped fidgeting but looked impatiently at Mary, who had followed her sister and was tugging at Sarah's hand.

Ben patted Sarah's head. "You can play with Mary in a few minutes," he said. "All these people want to say hi to you."

When the line tapered off, Jan relaxed. Many people shared positive responses. Jan was even learning some names. Finally, the last person shook her hand, and as she turned to Ben, standing beside her, the man who had glared at her during her sermon approached. He was tall, lanky, sixty-ish, and one of the few men in the church dressed in the traditional black suit, starched white shirt, and dark tie. The small woman who had been sitting next to him, flittered behind him, wringing her hands.

"Pastor Hendricks," he said in a commanding voice, "my name is John Tully, and I'm the treasurer of this church. Been the treasurer for over ten years."

Jan smiled and reached for his hand. "Hi John, I've looked forward…" She stopped as John snarled.

"Where in the Bible does it say women can preach?"

Shocked, Jan drew in a sharp breath and glanced at Ben, whose mouth had dropped open. When she found her voice, she could only utter, "Where does it say they can't?"

John walked away muttering, "I thought so." The petite woman briefly glanced into Jan's eyes before scrambling after him.

Jan put her hand on her chest, her heart racing. Heat flushed her face. Her worst nightmare, not being accepted because of her gender, was coming true. John Tully was the treasurer, an important leader, and he was already against her. *God, what am I going to do?*

Ben put his arm around her and murmured, "It'll be okay."

Betty Smith hurried up to them. She must have witnessed the exchange between Jan and John. "Don't mind him, Pastor Jan." She ushered them out of the sanctuary. "John's a little grumpy. He'll come around. Nobody else feels that way. You just don't even worry about this. Here, let me take your robe and I'll put it in your study. You go on and visit with the folks." She took Jan's robe and shooed them toward the fellowship hall where refreshments awaited.

Jan took Ben's hand. The earlier glow from the service vanished. She breathed deeply, trying to slow her heart rate. *How do I do this when people won't even give me a chance, just because I'm a woman?*

Ben squeezed her hand. "You can do this," he said.

"I sure hope so," she said, but she was shaken to her core. She wondered how many others sitting in the church, listening to her sermon a few minutes ago, felt the same way John did. Pastoring this church was not going to be easy. In fact, she was going to have to fight hard to even be considered having the authority she needed.

Jan clutched Ben's hand as they entered the fellowship hall.

Chapter Five

Jan hummed under her breath as she walked to the church the first week in July. The last few weeks had gone well and people were responding to her sermons and her pastoral care. The house was slowly becoming their home, thanks mostly to Ben. The backyard swing was getting great use as the girls were spending every minute with Wanda and Mary Williams. Jan's excitement grew as she contemplated ministry in this town.

Betty was shuffling some envelopes on her desk when Jan entered the office. The secretary was in her late fifties, short and round, with close-cropped grayish-brown hair and a puffy face. Always bubbly and smiling, she had been the secretary for First Church over twenty years. She had seen seven pastors come and go. And being a native of Baylorsville, she knew everyone. Setting the envelopes down, Betty frowned and scratched her head. She looked up at Jan.

"Anything wrong, Betty?" Jan asked.

"Yeah, John Tully must have been by last night and left the paychecks for me, the organist, the nursery attendant, and our custodian, but I don't see yours." She shuffled through the envelopes again.

"Does John normally leave all the checks on your desk at the beginning of the month?" This would be Jan's first paycheck. She had been given the details of her salary package before she started. She would be paid on the first of the month along with her four part-time staff members. "Maybe he left mine on my desk."

Jan walked into her study and looked on her desk. Unease gnawed at her. *Perhaps John isn't over his tirade.* "No, it's not here, Betty. Would he have left it anywhere else?"

"Don't think so," Betty said. "I'll just call him and see where he put it."

Jan got a strange, sinking feeling as Betty dialed the number. A throbbing started in the center of her forehead. She walked to the door between the two offices and listened.

"John, I've got the report of the offerings for June right here," Betty said, looking up at Jan and frowning. "It looks like we took in more money in June than in May."

Jan stepped into the office. The throbbing in her head intensified. "Let me talk to him."

Betty handed her the phone.

Putting it to her ear, Jan asked, "What's going on, John?"

"Uh, Pastor Hendricks," John said in a clipped, sarcastic tone, "it seems we don't have enough money to pay you this month. You're going to have to wait until this Sunday's offering for your paycheck."

"Just a minute." Jan struggled to keep her voice steady, the pain in her forehead really throbbing now. "I see the reports on the offering each week and I've also seen the reports from our May offerings. We're taking in more than enough money to cover salaries and our bills." Jan's heart was racing, and her face was turning red. She turned away from Betty. Did John have the audacity to withhold her paycheck just to prove, as the church treasurer, he held that authority over her? *How dare he do this!*

"Well, I'm the treasurer and have been for the two pastors before you, and I decide when and how to write the checks," John said in a smug tone. "You'll have to wait until next Monday." He hung up.

Jan slammed the phone down, ran her hand through her

hair, and collapsed into one of the office chairs. She looked up into Betty's startled face.

"What'd he say, Pastor Jan?"

Breathing deeply, Jan massaged her temple, trying to stay calm. "That we didn't have the money, and I wouldn't get paid until after the offering comes in for this Sunday." The withholding of her paycheck was a power play, and Jan needed to handle this right. If she got defensive, John would win.

"But we have the money. He can't do that, can he?" Betty asked.

"No, he can't, Betty." Jan's heart was racing. She knew she needed to do something and thought about calling the district superintendent but nixed that idea. She didn't want her boss to rescue her. Finally, she decided to call Nancy White, her staff parish chair. The staff parish committee was supposed to handle problems between the church and the pastor. And though it was risky calling Nancy, because John was a long-time church member and Jan didn't want problems to develop between Nancy and John, Jan needed to take a stand. She could not let John bully her about anything, especially her paycheck. Yes, calling Nancy was the right move. Jan took another deep breath, pushed the panicked thoughts out of her head, and got out of the chair.

"Don't worry about this, Betty. I'll call Nancy. She'll get this straightened out."

"I'm sorry, Pastor Jan. John can be a bully at times. Hope you get this worked out," Betty said, turning back to the typewriter.

"I'll get it worked out, Betty." *Or at least I hope I will.*

Jan went back into her study and shut the door, picking up the phone. Nancy was stunned and even sounded a little embarrassed. She assured Jan that she would speak with John.

Before the week was done, Jan had her paycheck. But involving Nancy, she had challenged John, and now the battle would really begin. How would this action affect the little authority Jan had managed to attain in this church and town?

Chapter Six

A week later, Jan was loading the dishwasher after dinner, thinking about her upcoming visit with the Tully family later on that night. She had wondered if the Tullys would cancel when she had called for confirmation that morning, but Martha had assured her the visit was expected. This had surprised Jan because of John's tirade with her paycheck. Jan was afraid it would be a difficult visit, and she was ticking off how to approach the conversation when Ben came up behind her, putting his arms around her. She turned into his hug and kissed him on the cheek.

"You going anywhere tonight?" he asked.

"Yeah, I've got a visit lined up." She closed the dishwasher and started the cycle, knowing she had to make this visit, but wishing she could skip it. As she turned back around to face Ben, she noticed the lines around his mouth, suggesting he was not happy.

He confirmed that when he said, "Sure seems you've been spending lots of hours at the church, then visiting families every night. Don't you think you need to spend time with the girls?"

Jan grew irritated. She was already dreading this visit, and now Ben was challenging her. Why couldn't he understand that she had to be present one hundred percent with the church, which meant putting in many hours? And she sure couldn't cancel this visit. What would John think? He already didn't think she should be the pastor. She grabbed a rag off the sink and slapped at the counters.

"Ben, it's important that I get to know these people." A wave of guilt flashed over her; her family needed her too.

A little over a month had passed since her arrival. In that time, she had visited twelve families, eight shut-ins, three people in two hospitals in Tallahassee, and was teaching an adult Sunday school class. And plans were also in place for a leaders' retreat in the fall. Plus, she was preaching every Sunday, something she hadn't been doing in her previous church. It was exhausting. She remembered the advice of a clergywoman friend who said women had to work twice as hard as male pastors.

Jan threw the rag in the sink and slumped in a kitchen chair.

Ben sat in a chair beside her. "Jan, you're doing a great job. These people already love you. But you can't work 24/7. And you need to be with the girls some. They're in a strange place. Even if I don't find work right away, we're still in this parenting thing together."

She glanced into the den where the girls were coloring, and the guilt returned. She couldn't remember the last time she had taken part in their bedtime rituals of bath and reading. "I know I'm spending a lot of time working, but I've got so much to do."She looked at him. "I want so much for this church to like me." Tears trickled down her cheek, which surprised her. She brushed at them. "But I have to prove I'm just as good, if not better, than the men."

He leaned over and gave her a peck on the cheek. "You're so much better than you think. But you can't continue to be a good pastor if you don't feed your soul. You've got to balance. You need time for you and us."

Sighing deeply, Jan put her head on the table. Ben was right. She needed time for rest, reflection, and her family. But she also needed to prove to her congregation that she could be their pastor. "I know. It's just so hard gauging how I'm doing as pastor."

"You're doing fine." He lifted her head up and brushed her hair away from her face. "Tomorrow is Friday, your day off. Let's go to Tallahassee and spend time at the mall. The girls need school clothes, and you need to get away. We can have dinner in town."

Jan smiled. "Can we go to that Southern-style country restaurant?"

He laughed and hugged her. "Sure. By the way, who're you seeing tonight?"

"The Tullys," Jan said, avoiding his eyes.

Ben raised his eyebrows. "Are you sure you should go out there by yourself?"

Jan reached for her purse lying on the kitchen counter. "Yeah, I'll be fine. They did sign up for this meeting."

"Well, be careful. Sounds like John Tully wants to make trouble. That deal with your paycheck was no laughing matter."

"Oh, as Betty says, he's just a bully. I can handle him. Bye girls." She blew them a kiss. *At least I hope I can.*

The Tully family lived north of town, almost in Georgia. Jan was glad the sun didn't set until after 9:00 in late July. She needed the extra light to find the turnoff. She followed a long, winding clay dirt road, laughing to herself as she remembered other directions her church members had given her. "You go down to the end of the lane and take a left at the big oak tree and then a right at the fence." At least the directions to the Tullys were a bit easier.

It was beautiful here. Jan put the windows down and breathed in the sweet scent of the pine forest. In this part of the state, limbs from giant oak trees grew across the road to form canopies. The setting sun caused little light explosions along the way. On the side of the road, a large white bird, some kind of crane, stared into the grass, waiting to snap its beak on an unsuspecting insect. Her nervousness lessened as she took in the scenery.

Approaching the Tullys' house, though, her heart rate increased. *Maybe I shouldn't have come here by myself.* But she brushed off that thought as she came up to a large ranch-style brick house. She parked the car and got out as John's wife, Martha, opened the front door to the wrap-around porch. Martha was a small woman. But she appeared shriveled, not petite. Gray wisps of hair circled her small face. She was wearing a long, old-fashioned dress with an apron.

"Hi, Martha," Jan said, climbing the porch steps. "Thanks for inviting me over." But when Jan noticed Martha wringing her hands and not meeting her eyes, she realized something was not quite right.

"I'm so sorry you came all the way out here, Pastor Jan," Martha said. "John, uh…. had to go over to a neighbor's house to fix a broken pipe. It, it happened quite suddenly. I thought about calling, but realized you were probably on the way. I'm so sorry."

Yeah, right, he's probably in the den right now. "Oh, that's okay, Martha, how about the two of us talk?"

"Um, no, I would rather wait until John is here."

"I could talk with him later, but how about you and I visit here on the porch swing?" She sensed Martha wanted to talk and the pastoral voice inside urged her to probe further.

"No, um, Pastor Jan, I really think John should be here, too." Martha wiped at her eyes and nervously looked behind her.

Jan did a slow burn. She had driven all this way when she could've been with her family. And John and Martha had signed up for this visit. She wondered why Martha wouldn't talk to her without John. Something was going on and Jan needed to pursue it, but she didn't think she could probe any further right now. She wondered if it was Martha's nervousness that made her want to leave, or Jan's own lack of courage. Secretly, she was glad the confrontation with John would be put off, although she was a bit miffed that she was being turned away. After all, Martha did confirm the visit this morning.

"That's okay, Martha, we can certainly do this later. Please tell John I'm sorry I missed him. Hope to see you in church this week." She turned and walked back down the steps toward the car.

"Pastor Jan."

Jan turned back to Martha.

"Thanks for coming." Martha looked right into Jan's eyes. Jan saw something there.

"Good night, Martha," Jan said, getting into her car.

Driving back down the long road, Jan wondered what had just happened. John obviously didn't like her. But why? Was it the woman issue or a power issue? She knew the paycheck event certainly suggested an authority issue. Jan was frustrated. She didn't have time to play games with John. She had too many other people to attend to. And Martha's attitude puzzled her. Was that fear, or sadness she had seen in her eyes? But Jan was too tired, and it was too late to figure that out now. At some point she would have to confront them both. But not tonight. She was going home to her family. She smiled to herself. *Maybe I'll get home in time to read to the girls.*

Chapter Seven

It was a week after Jan's failed attempt to visit the Tullys, and Jan had managed to put John Tully's strange behavior out of her mind. Today, she was thinking about Ben. He had finally heard from Tallahassee Community College and was being interviewed this morning. Jan hoped he would get the job, but worried how they could make their two jobs work. Tallahassee was an hour away. What if one of the girls got sick and both she and Ben were out of town?

She was cleaning up after lunch when Ben's car pulled into the carport. Her heart rate picked up. The girls had gone to their rooms to rest and read before heading over to the Williamses to play. She hadn't heard from Ben since he'd left that morning and feared the news was not good. She looked up as he entered the kitchen. Ben's beaming smile told her the interview had gone well.

"You're looking at the new Humanities professor at Tallahassee Community College," he exclaimed, grabbing her around the waist and twirling her around the kitchen. "I start the end of August and will teach three beginning courses!"

"Wow, that's great!" Jan squealed. "Put me down, you'll hurt yourself."

"Yeah, it's more than I thought I would teach. Only problem is, two classes are during the day, on Monday, Wednesday, and

Friday, and one is on Tuesday night. And the night class is three hours, from six to nine. That means I'll be gone at least four days a week." Ben opened the refrigerator and started pulling out items to make a sandwich.

Jan watched him, beginning to panic. "Ben, I'm happy for you, but what about childcare? Tallahassee is an hour away."

Ben took the sandwich makings to the kitchen table, poured iced tea from the pitcher into a glass and looked up at her. "Well, we're going to have to be creative about childcare. My first class doesn't start until ten, so I don't have to be at the school until nine. That means I'll be leaving about the same time the girls need to be at school, so I can help with all of that." He took a big bite of his sandwich and quickly chewed. "Unfortunately, my next class on those days isn't until two, so I probably won't be home until about four, maybe four-thirty. I'll do office hours between the two classes and late Tuesday afternoons, so I'll go in about three on Tuesdays and stay home on Thursdays and work from here." He took a big gulp of tea, looked up at her and grinned. "We can do this."

Jan couldn't help but laugh. "You seem to have figured this all out on the way home." She kissed him on the top of his head and sat down beside him. "I'm excited for you. Teaching Humanities is your thing. But I didn't expect you to be able to teach that many classes your first year. That's more than you taught in Tampa."

"Yep, but Tallahassee Community College, or TCC, as they call it, has a big freshmen class this year and Humanities is one of the basic courses. I'm basically full time."

Jan smiled at him, but she began to panic again. She wanted him to get a job, but full time in Tallahassee seemed a bit much.

"Hey, what's up, your eyes are glazing over?"

Jan looked up to see Ben peering at her. She sighed. "I am happy for you, but how're we going to work this out? What about Tuesday nights? I usually have meetings that night."

"Well, looks like we'll have to find a babysitter."

"But we don't know anyone here. How're we going to find one we can trust?"

Jan noticed Ben's excited chatter quieting as he looked down at his sandwich. *He's getting angry, I don't want him to be angry.*

He finally looked up. "Jan, you knew I'd be looking for a job. And we could use this money." He took another swallow of tea, balled up his napkin, and took her hand. "What's really going on here?"

Jan squeezed his hand and sighed. "Of course, I wanted you to get this job, but I've got so much to do and I just don't see how we can manage. You're going to be so far away. What if the girls get sick? What if I have an emergency and there's no one to pick up the girls? What if…?"

Ben pulled his hand away from hers, his eyes beginning their annoyance tic. "Then we'll work it out. We did this in Tampa all the time. One of us will stay home, or we'll get a babysitter."

"Yeah, but here the thinking is that you'll go to work and I'll stay home, and if I stay home, then the church will assume I'm not pulling my weight as their pastor."

Ben slapped his hand on the table. "Good grief, Jan, what's going on? This isn't about me getting this job, it's about you worried you can't or won't be accepted in yours." He got up and paced around the kitchen table.

Jan watched him, feeling guilty. "I'm sorry," she said lowering her eyes. "I am happy about your new job. I'm just so worried about mine."

"So, what brought this on?" Ben stopped pacing and sat back down, facing her.

Jan looked right into Ben's eyes. "I had a conversation with a woman yesterday who asked me what I was going to do with the children when you found a job and started to work."

"What'd you tell her?" Ben asked.

"That we'd work it out. But I worried she was subtly telling me I shouldn't be working when the girls are still so little, or even that women shouldn't be doing what I'm doing."

"Why do you read so much into what people say? Maybe she was trying to see if you needed childcare." Ben tilted her chin toward him. "Jan, I believe in you. But you've got to stop worrying about what people think. You need to believe in yourself." He got up and kissed her on the forehead. "I'm going to change and then take the girls to get ice cream. I want to celebrate. Want to come?"

Ben headed down the hallway. "Hey, girls, who wants ice cream?"

Jan stared at him. *I'm being a jerk. God, help me.* She wondered why she let what people said bother her so much.

As excited cries came from the back of the house, Jan slowly got up. She sighed deeply as the girls bounded into the kitchen chattering about what flavor of ice cream they would get. *Perhaps it's because I feel like all of us are in a fishbowl.* She followed Ben out of the house. Ice cream sounded nice.

Chapter *Eight*

"Mom, Mom, get up, it's time to get up."

Jan opened her eyes to see Carrie and Sarah dancing around her bedroom. It was still dark out.

Ben groaned. "What time is it?"

Jan rolled over and looked at the alarm clock. The bright red numbers read 6:00 a.m. She rubbed her eyes. "Girls, it's not time to get up yet. School doesn't start until 8:30." It was the first day of school, third grade for Carrie and kindergarten for Sarah.

"But Mom," Carrie said, "Wanda and Mary will be ready by 8:00 and we want to walk to school together."

"Well, you have plenty of time to get ready by 8:00. And I'm walking with you this morning since it's the first day." Jan got out of bed and put on her robe. "Come on, I'll make pancakes."

"Wow, pancakes, I'll get up for that, too," Ben said.

Ben had been at his job for a full week, getting ready for classes starting right after Labor Day. A childcare plan had been agreed on. Sarah and Carrie would stay at the aftercare program run by the school. Either Jan or Ben would pick them up by 5:30. They would work out sickness and appointments when the need arose.

Thank you, God, for this beautiful morning, for the girls' first day, for Ben's new job, for this place and this time. Jan continued to pray as she stirred the pancake batter and turned on the burner.

Things were working out. Life was good. *This is amazing grace.* A thought burst into her head. That would be a great title for her sermon this week. She would talk about the incredible grace of God who acts in people's lives even when they don't see it.

As Jan set the plates of pancakes on the table, the girls, dressed for school, climbed on their chairs. Jan smiled as she saw Sarah's shirt on backward.

"Hold on a minute little one, let me turn that around for you."She took advantage of holding on to Sarah to brush her long, blond hair and put it up in a ponytail.

"Where's your ribbon?" she asked.

Sarah reached in her pocket and handed it to her mom. She took a big bite of her pancakes.

"Don't get any syrup on you," Jan said.

Carrie was wearing new white shorts and a red top. She, too, had a ribbon in her hair, but Carrie's hair was shorter, barely able to hold a ponytail, brown and a bit wispy. Jan marveled that her children looked so different from one another.

"Good luck girls," Ben said, grabbing a dry pancake and his cup of coffee as he raced through the kitchen. He kissed both of them on the cheek and headed toward the kitchen door. "I can't wait to hear about your first day of school. See you this afternoon." With his briefcase in his hand, he stepped into the carport.

Jan got ready herself, and they walked the short distance to the elementary school, picking up Wanda, Mary and their mom, Linda, along the way.

"Carrie and Sarah are so looking forward to starting school," Jan said as the four girls skipped ahead and Jan and Linda fell in behind. Wanda, though, seemed lethargic and dragged her feet. "Looks like Wanda didn't sleep too well last night. Was she too excited to sleep?"

With a worried expression, Linda stopped. "Pastor Jan, I'm getting worried about Wanda. She just isn't right. She fell asleep again yesterday afternoon and just doesn't seem to be her perky self. I hope she can make it through the day."

Jan stopped too and looked at Linda. Lines etched across her forehead and her lips quivered, as she watched the girls walking ahead of them. A trickle of unease ran through Jan. She took Linda's hand. "How long has she been this way?"

"She started feeling puny about a month ago. I thought it was just the heat, and she needed to play quieter games indoors, but when she began wanting to take naps in the afternoons, I got worried. She hasn't napped since she was in diapers."

"I hope she's not sick. I'll keep her in my prayers."

"Thanks, Pastor Jan. I've made a doctor's appointment for her next week. She's so excited about school. I hope she'll be alright."

They resumed following the children to school. Jan hoped Wanda was okay, too. She was a sweet child, and Carrie had already claimed her as her best friend.

After getting everyone settled in their rooms and saying hi to several church members also escorting their children to school, Jan walked back to the house with Linda. She said goodbye to her and walked toward the church. As she passed the lake, she decided to pray and walk around it for a couple of laps.

Lord God, be with all of the children and teachers as they begin this school year. Help my Carrie and Sarah have a good day, especially Sarah as she begins her school journey. And I pray Wanda's okay. Embrace her in your arms and surround her with your healing touch. Amen.

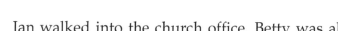

Jan walked into the church office. Betty was already there, working on the attendance pads. Jan sniffed the deep, acrid scent of coffee and sighed. "Oh, Betty, you are amazing, thanks for getting this started." She picked up a chipped green cup and filled it with the hot brew. "Just what I needed."

"You're welcome. By the way, great service yesterday. Looks like we had a good attendance and a solid offering."

Betty opened a closet door and bent down to the small safe

on the floor. Opening the safe, she said, "I'll run the offering over to the bank. Jim will meet me there and we'll count it. The girls get to school okay?" Betty had several grandchildren of her own and already treated Sarah and Carrie as her own.

"Yes, they seemed very excited. I think they'll enjoy this year. I like their teachers. It helps that I know Sarah's teacher, Shirley Thomas." Jan took her cup of coffee into her small study, connected to the church office by a door. Before she could sit down, Betty spoke.

"Oh, John Tully called right before you got here. He wants to come by this morning. I told him to come in at nine-thirty. Didn't see anything on your calendar for then. Hope that was okay?" she said walking out the office door with the offering.

"Thanks," Jan said. *Great. What does he want now?* After the conversation about her paycheck, and the strange visit with Martha, Jan had put them out of her mind, deciding to try connecting with them again sometime in late fall. They had not been back to church. Jan worried about John's agenda.

She heard a car door slam, and a garbled "Hi, John" from Betty in the parking lot. Apparently, John had arrived.

A moment later he walked into the church office, Martha following.

"Come in, John and Martha, please sit down," Jan said as she met them at her study door and ushered them in. "Would you like coffee?"

"Nope, won't be here long enough to drink it," John said. He didn't bother to sit. Martha fidgeted with her hands.

"What can I do for you today?" Jan sat, then stood, when John and Martha continued to stand.

"Just want to give you this." He thrust a piece of paper toward her. Jan took the paper but didn't read it.

"Says I'm resigning as Treasurer. Also says we're leaving the church."

Jan's stomach clenched. She saw Martha flinch. This decision to leave the church was not mutual.

"I'm sorry, John. Can we talk about this?" she stammered. Her face burned and her stomach churned. What was wrong with him, and what was wrong with her that she couldn't just confront him? *God, this man makes me so angry.*

"Nope. When I heard a woman was coming as our preacher, I didn't think I would like it. Now I know I don't. I was going to give it a couple of months but decided to go ahead and leave now." John paced back and forth and looked at the floor.

Jan's heart raced and the queasiness in her stomach increased. She tried in vain to remain calm and professional. Her mind blanked on all the stuff she learned in seminary about disgruntled church members.

"Well, John, I'm sorry you feel this way," she finally squeaked. "But if you're unhappy here, it might be a good thing for you to step out of the treasurer's position for now and give it some time."

"Time!" he yelled, as Jan flinched. "I don't need to give it time. I'm quitting now. Perhaps when you leave, I'll come back. There are others in this church and town who don't think you should be here. Why I bet you won't last five years being a preacher." With that, he grabbed Martha's hand and stormed out of the office. Martha was crying as Jan watched them leave through the window. Shaking, she sat down and put her head on her desk.

A tear slid down her cheek. She was glad that Betty hadn't been around to witness that exchange. Doubts surged through her head. Did other people feel the same way John did? Would there be a massive exodus from the church? Maybe she didn't have the skills it took to do this job. The fears of not being good enough, which had plagued her since childhood, surfaced with a jolt. She stopped and picked up the phone to call Ben.

When he answered, she sobbed, "I need to see you. Can I meet you in Tallahassee for an early lunch?" At his affirmative answer, she wrote a quick note to Betty saying she had to go out and rushed home to get the car, all the while praying for strength to handle this new crisis.

Chapter Nine

Jan's mind raced on the hour-long trip to the community college in Tallahassee. She alternated between crying, praying, and yelling about John. By the time she pulled into the parking lot of the college, she had calmed down. Ben was waiting for her on a bench outside the main building.

He got in on the passenger side, leaned over to give her a kiss, and said, "What's up?"

Her calmness dissolved, and she burst into tears.

"Whoa," Ben said. "Here, let me drive." Getting out, he went to the driver's side, opening the door and helping Jan out.

"Hey." He put his finger under her chin and kissed her on the cheek. "What's wrong?"

Jan threw her arms around him, still sobbing. "I don't know if I can do this," she stammered, hiccupping through her tears.

"Okay, relax, and tell me what happened." He held her tight a minute longer, then stepped back, glancing at the people in the parking lot staring at them. "Let's get in the car. We're creating a scene."

Jan brushed her hair away from her face and rubbed the tears from her eyes. "Okay." She climbed in the car, grabbed a tissue, and blew her nose.

"I'm sorry, Ben," she said when they had closed the car doors and he had started the car. "I thought I'd worked through this on the ride over." She grimaced and looked over at him. "Guess I hadn't."

"Obviously not. Must've been something pretty bad since you drove all the way over here." He peered at her, a worried expression on his face. "The girls are okay, aren't they?"

"Oh, yeah, they're fine. This isn't about them."

"Good. So, do you want to talk here, or get some lunch?

"Let's get lunch. I feel like that country place, Po' Folks. Need comfort food and some good sweet iced tea."

On the way to the restaurant, Jan shared with Ben the details of the conversation she had had with John. He listened without interrupting. Ben had attended Duke Divinity School, too, but had concentrated on pastoral care. After a year, though, he decided to pursue his love of Humanities. But he still had great insights, and Jan trusted his instincts.

They entered the restaurant and made their way to a quiet, corner booth. After ordering iced tea and food, Ben responded.

"Sounds like John's a bully. I'd say good riddance to him." Ben gulped his tea.

"Yes, he's a bully, but I should be able to handle him. And I'm furious that I can't confront him."

Their food came, fried chicken for Ben and baked tilapia for her. Ben chewed his food, his brow wrinkling. He finally swallowed and said, "Well, maybe your problem today is more about you than John."

Jan snickered, "You should've been a therapist."

Suddenly she slammed her fork down and swiped at the tears, which had started again. "My temper just flares when he attacks me. I get so defensive and I don't want to be that way."

Ben placed his hand over hers and looked into her eyes. "Okay, so why are you so defensive? What are you really afraid of?"

Jan sighed and looked down at her food. She squeezed his hand, picked up her fork and toyed with her fish. "I guess it's the same stuff I've always been afraid of, that I can't cut it as a woman pastor. I get so intimidated by people who yell at me, especially men, and certainly John. I can't seem to separate whether he's yelling at me as a person, or me as a woman, or even me as the pastor of the church."

Ben waited while the waitress refilled his tea. "I think you being afraid of not cutting it as a pastor and your anger at John are connected. Perhaps your problem with John is just a reflection of your fear."

"Wow, you really are being the therapist." Jan pushed her barely touched fish away from her and sipped her tea.

"Think about this," Ben continued, "you're probably being too hard on yourself as a woman pastor. You've only been at this church a few months. All pastors have a tough time the first year."

"But women have it…" Jan interrupted, but Ben waved her off as he sat up straighter and looked into her eyes.

"Let me finish. I know it's different as a woman and you've got a lot more pressure to succeed than the male pastors, but some problems are the same. John is testing you to see if you'll give in to him. Yes, he's a bully, and yes, he probably isn't too keen on having a woman as a pastor. And for sure, there's something else going on, and sometime, you'll have to figure that out, but he's testing you, just like he would test a new male pastor."

"But…" Jan tried to interrupt again, but Ben shushed her.

"You're getting defensive. You need to slow down a little and do things that help feed your soul. Like I said the other week, you're working way too many hours. You haven't taken a day off since we went school shopping. You've got to figure out a way to balance your job and your personal life, or you'll burn out."

Jan fiddled with her glass, tears filling her eyes again.

Ben reached over to her and brushed the tears away. "I'm not trying to be mean, but don't you remember what you learned in Tampa about setting boundaries and carving out space for yourself?" Ben sighed. "And for me and the girls?"

Jan thought back to her time in Tampa. As a young clergy-woman, and the first woman pastor in that large church, Jan felt pressure to excel. Carrie was a little over two years old when she started as the associate pastor, and Jan felt she had to be the best pastor, the best wife, and the best mother. She ended up not being the best of anything. Things went well the first year, but by the second year, Jan had grown tired and edgy. Working over fifty hours a week and trying to be a full-time mom to Carrie and a good wife to Ben had not been pretty. During her third year in Tampa, she had gotten pregnant with Sarah and realized things needed to change. After the birth and while still on maternity leave, she attended a woman's retreat and found the resources, support, and spiritual strength to manage her time and set boundaries within her family and the church. She took her days off, slowed down on the evening activities, and managed to do more family activities together on Saturdays.

She looked up at Ben. "Yeah, I guess I wasn't so good those first few years. But I needed to prove that I... that women... could do this."

Ben slapped his hand on the table, which made Jan jump. "But that's the point, Jan. You don't need to prove that you, or any other woman, can succeed as a pastor. You're already doing it. You've already done it. You don't need to relearn how to balance everything. You just need to do it." Ben rubbed his hand. "Sorry, didn't mean to do that." He laughed. "Owww, that hurt."

Jan took his hand and kissed it. "Okay, you've made your case."

"Well, what're you going to do about this?"

The waitress brought the bill, they paid and headed out of the restaurant. Jan went to the car while Ben stopped at the restroom. He joked he didn't want to get up in the middle of the faculty meeting to relieve himself. Waiting for Ben, she thought about what he had said. *What am I going to do about this?*

***

After dropping Ben off at the college, Jan headed home, thinking about the conversation with Ben. Those first few years in Tampa had been rough. But after the birth of Sarah and the clergywomen retreat, she had learned how to balance her work and her family time. She needed to put that in place here.

And Ben was right about the issue with John being more about her than him. She slapped the steering wheel. John had problems but she couldn't let his problems be her problems.

As she turned off the interstate, she mentally listed the things that needed to change in her life; a daily prayer time, cutting back on night visitations, scheduling date nights now that Ben was working, and certainly walking around her 'sanctuary' lake, which calmed and fortified her. This church didn't need her twenty-four hours a day. Perhaps she could make a list at the beginning of the week with all of her duties. She could do a little each day so she wouldn't get so frantic at the end of the week. She would also make sure she got home in time to share the cooking responsibilities with Ben on the nights he was home. Yes, she was going to take care of herself, and that would help her take care of the church, and even deal with bullies like John.

Coming to the only red light in town, she looked at her watch. School was just getting out. Her original plans were for the girls to stay in the aftercare program until 5:00. But on a whim, she turned the car around and headed to the school. She would pick them up and take them to Hardee's for ice cream. She smiled to herself as she parked in the school lot. She could do her job. John would still be a problem and there would be problems with others, but yes, she would excel as the pastor of this church. She got out of the car and went to find the girls. She couldn't wait to see how their day went.

Chapter Ten

Two days later Jan was working on her sermon in her study. She had shared with Ben the decisions she had made to discipline her life. And Jan had every intention to keep to this schedule, which, hopefully, would improve the way she handled difficult issues. She felt centered and even energized.

The phone rang and a moment later, Betty knocked on the door. "Pastor Jan, it's Julie, Winnie Mae's daughter." Julie and her mother were lifelong members of the church. Winnie Mae had recently had a heart attack and was recovering in a rehab center in Tallahassee. Jan had visited her several times and enjoyed chatting about the history of the town and the church.

Jan picked up the phone. "Hello, Julie, what can I do for you?"

"Pastor Jan," Julie's voice shook, "my mom has had another heart attack. They've taken her by ambulance to the hospital in Tallahassee. I'm on my way there now."

Jan's heart sank. This did not sound good. Her voice shook as she fought to stay calm. "Oh, no, I'm so sorry. I'll meet you there." She got her purse and went into the front office.

"Winnie Mae has had another heart attack," Jan told Betty as she headed out the door. "Start the prayer chain. And can you call Ben and tell him I may be late today? Have him pick up the girls."

Jan ran home to get the car. Winnie Mae, in her late eighties, was a delightful southern woman who could tell some wonderful stories of the early days of Baylorsville. And she was a strong Christian and had been a single parent, who had brought up her daughter, Julie, and two nephews. Jan truly loved Winnie Mae. After every visit, Jan came away feeling stronger and somehow more connected with God.

O God, be with Winnie Mae, she prayed as she got into her car and for the second time that week took the hour-long trip to Tallahassee. *Surround her with your grace, your hope, and your light. And be with her family as they gather. Amen.*

Jan pulled into the hospital parking lot and parked in clergy parking. As she closed the door, an elderly man, who had just parked, approached her.

"Excuse me, miss, but this parking is for clergy only. You need to move your car."

Jan sighed and said in an exasperated tone, "I am clergy. Here is my clergy card."

She thrust the badge, which was around her neck, toward him and took off. It was getting old that people assumed she wasn't clergy just because she was a woman.

She found Julie and her cousins, John and Mike, in the Emergency Room. They had seen Winnie Mae but were waiting now while the doctors were attending to her. Jan sat beside the solemn family members.

"Doesn't look too good, Pastor," John said. "She had to be resuscitated in the ambulance and now her blood pressure is dropping."

John, in his fifties, was the oldest of the cousins. He had been ten when Winnie Mae had taken him and his brother, Mike, to live with her when their parents were both sent to jail. Jan had heard the sad story of his childhood from both him and Winnie Mae. He was devoted to Winnie Mae and was heartbroken when she had had her first heart attack. He wanted her to have surgery to put stints in her heart to help with blood flow, but the doctors felt the surgery was too much for her frail body.

"We should have forced the doctor to do surgery on her," John said, his voice coming in punctuated sharp whispers. "She wouldn't have had this second heart attack." He jumped up and paced around the small waiting room.

Julie raised her head, which had been in her hands, and looked up at her cousin. "John, we talked about this. Mom didn't want the surgery."

Mike, four years John's junior, stood and placed his hands on his brother's shoulders, stopping him from pacing. "John, she probably wouldn't have made it through surgery. Besides, even if she had had the surgery, she would have been in pain. At least she didn't suffer the last few weeks."

John shook his head and resumed his pacing.

Jan watched and listened to the cousins' agonizing conversation. Knowing they needed to release their pain and frustration, she let them talk while she silently prayed. After they were quiet for a few minutes, she stood and motioned for them to hold hands. "Let's pray".

"God, you know what Winnie Mae needs. Surround her with your love. Be with the doctors and nurses who are helping her. And be with Julie, John and Mike, and the rest of the family. Amen."

Ten minutes later, a nurse came and led them into Winnie Mae's small emergency room cubicle. Winnie Mae lay pale and unmoving on the bed with her eyes closed. The nurse bustled around fiddling with the tubes running into Winnie Mae's arms, but Jan could tell the medicine flowing through her body was not helping. Julie's eyes filled with tears as the heart monitor sitting beside the bed slowly stopped beeping. Mike bent over his aunt's body and kissed her on the cheek, while John and Julie grabbed Winnie Mae's hands. Jan silently prayed as Winnie Mae died.

This would be Jan's first funeral in Baylorsville. She had done several in the past as the associate pastor in her previous church and was comfortable doing funerals, but this one was different. Winnie Mae and her family had become close friends, and Jan was mourning her death too. And a lot was at stake. Jan pulled up in front of Winnie Mae's house and remembered Dr. Sayer, her worship professor in Seminary, saying that the first funeral in a new church was a deal-breaker for the preacher. Not only would her church members be looking at how she conducted herself with the service and the family, but the whole town would, too. Generations of Winnie Mae's family had lived in Baylorsville, and Jan expected a packed church. She knocked on the door and prayed silently. *Oh God, help me comfort this family. And comfort me, too. And please don't let me mess up!*

Jan walked into the living room of Julie's house where about twenty family members and the two funeral directors, Bob Mullens and his assistant, Jim Long, were gathered as they waited for funeral home cars. These would take them to the church for the funeral and then to the cemetery for the burial.

"Friends, I'm so sorry for your loss. Winnie Mae was a wonderful person. It was my privilege to have known her. I loved her deeply. Let's hold hands and pray together before we leave.

"Lord God, you know the pain of this family. Hold them in your arms as they go through this service. Remind them that Winnie Mae is safe and in your loving arms, and also remind them they are not alone. You are there with them. Amen." She squeezed Julie's hand as they made their way to the cars.

As Jan got into her car, which was in front of the funeral coach, Bob Mullens came up to her and quietly said, "You've been so wonderful with this family. I know them and they have appreciated the care you have shown them."He smiled and shook her hand as he headed to the lead care for the funeral procession to the church.

Jan thought about that affirmation as the funeral procession headed to the church. *Thanks, God. At least I'm doing something right.*

Chapter Eleven

"Mom, I want to be a witch for Halloween," Carrie said at dinner one night around the middle of October.

"Me, too," Sarah piped in. Both girls riveted their eyes on Jan for approval.

"Why do you want to be witches?" Jan asked.

"They're scary and everyone's going to be one," Carrie said.

Jan looked at Ben, and he covered his mouth to hide a laugh. But Jan found no humor in the girls wanting to be witches. What would people say if the daughters of the Methodist pastor dressed up as witches for Halloween? Jan didn't want to find out. She wondered how she could change their minds.

"Hmm, if everyone's going as a witch, no one will be able to tell you apart. Do you want to look like everyone else?"

Carrie squinted her eyes and scrunched her nose. "Oh," she said as she picked up her glass of milk. "But I still want to be a witch. Everyone's going to be witches." And she proceeded to finish her drink as if this sealed the deal.

"Yes, everyone's going to be witches." Sarah liked mimicking everything Carrie said.

Ben laughed, and both girls looked at him. "Well, I guess you'll be witches like everyone else." The girls both clapped their hands.

"Ben, don't encourage them." Jan's voice was louder than she intended and both girls stopped clapping and stared at her. Jan got up and cleared the table, noticing Ben, too, was watching her with a puzzled expression. She didn't want to get into this with him. *Ben doesn't understand.* Not only would the church and town think she was a terrible mom if the children went as witches, but they would also question her role as pastor.

"What's wrong with them going as witches?" Ben asked. "They'd make cute witches in their little black pointed hats." He got up and tickled Sarah, and both girls laughed. "Okay, witches, go get your bath and get ready for bed."

Jan set the dishes on the counter and ran her hand through her hair, watching the girls head toward the back of the house. "Ben, what will the church and town think? They're the children of the Methodist preacher." She leaned against the counter. She thought about the whispers, phone calls, and stares from the congregation and the town. "They just can't be witches."

"Whoa, where did that come from, Jan?" Ben said. He brought more dishes to the kitchen. "Halloween's a fun children's holiday. And if I remember correctly, you and I attended a school Halloween party as a witch and a devil." He smiled as he, too, leaned against the counter. "That was a great party."

"This isn't funny, Ben." Jan's voice cracked. She started to pace in the small kitchen, bumping into him. "This town is very conservative. The church is very conservative. You remember what happened to my friend in central Florida last year. He put a picture of a black cat on the front door of his parsonage for Halloween and his trustee chair nearly ripped his head off and made him take it down." Jan grabbed a plate and almost threw it into the dishwasher. "Members of his church complained he was getting into black magic. What if the church and town think we are into black magic, or the occult, if we let our kids go as witches for Halloween?"

Ben grabbed her shoulder and turned her around. "Good grief, Jan? Black magic… the occult? Tell me you don't believe that?" He lifted her chin with his finger. "What's really going on?"

Jan's voice caught, and a tear rolled down her face. "I'm so scared that every move I make is being watched by everyone."

"Jan, a lot of that's your perception. You're doing a great job here. The people love you. The girls being witches for Halloween will not change that, especially if, as our daughters so emphatically said, everyone is going as witches." He kissed her forehead as the "witches" came running down the hall in their pajamas.

"Daddy, it's your turn to read us the story," Sarah said, thrusting a copy of *The Wizard of Oz* into his hands.

"Yeah, Daddy, we're at the good part about Glenda, the good witch," Carrie said, as they pulled Ben into the den.

Ben looked back at Jan and mouthed, "We'll talk later," and settled onto the couch to read to his two little girls.

Jan finished loading the dishwasher. *God, what am I doing? What's wrong with me?* She pinched her nose to stop her sudden headache. *Why does this bother me so much?* She was wiping off the table when she heard the girls laugh. Going to the door between the kitchen and the den, she watched her family. Sarah wiggled closer to Ben so she could see the pictures. Carrie's hand followed the words in the book.

"And Glenda, the good witch..." Ben said.

A light blinked on in Jan's head. The good witch. "Hey girls," she said coming into the den and perching on the arm of the couch.

The girls looked up as Ben stopped reading.

"How about being the good witch, Glenda, from *The Wizard of Oz* for Halloween?" Jan said rubbing her hands together. "You could still be witches, but you wouldn't be the same as everyone else." Jan was on a roll. "I bet Miss Emily could make you long blue dresses and I could get you a wand from the General Store."

Ben shook his head as he closed the book, but the girls got excited.

"Hey, that sounds cool," Carrie said, jumping down from the couch and twirling around. "Could we get crowns and sparkled shoes, too?"

"I like sparkled shoes," Sarah piped in, twirling in her sister's footsteps.

Ben smiled. "Well, I guess that settles it. Glenda, the good witch, it is. Now, off to bed, my good little witches."

Jan followed them to their bedrooms. They said prayers together, then Jan and Ben came back into the den.

Sitting in their La-Z-Boy chairs, Ben said, "Nice move about Glenda, the good witch, but I still don't understand why you got so upset about the girls wanting to be witches."

She laid her head back in the chair. "I'm sorry. I know I overreacted. But I'm worried what people will say. It's like I'm in a fishbowl, and all of you are too."

"Well, I'm definitely not in a fishbowl. I won't kowtow to anyone in this church or this town. I'm going to be me." He took her hand. "What set this off?"

Jan sighed. "Betty mentioned today that someone from the town asked her why I was so snobbish. Evidently, I didn't acknowledge this person while I was walking to the post office last week." Jan pounded the side of the chair with her other hand. "That made me so angry. I'm sure my thoughts were on the funeral for Winnie Mae. Why do I have to be 'up' all the time?"

Ben let go of her hand and lifted the footrest on the chair. "Why did Betty even mention that?"

"She's just trying to help me. She thinks if I know what people are saying about me, I can correct my mistakes. But that stuff makes me feel worse." Jan put up the footrest on her chair, too, and laid back. "I can't please everyone."

"No, you can't."

"I know, but getting back to the girls being witches, I thought I could prevent that from becoming an issue."

"Well, sounds like the girls are all right with being Glenda the Good Witch, and folks shouldn't have a problem with that. But Jan, you've got to stop worrying so much about what people are saying." He leaned over and took her hand again. "You need to believe in yourself and trust that God is with you. You did such a great job with the funeral. Lots of folks agreed. That's what you need to be listening to."

"Yeah, I guess you're right." She squeezed his hand. "Thanks. Sorry for blowing up." She let go of his hand and picked up a book as he turned on the TV. She was glad a compromise had been reached between her and Ben about the witch costumes, but she knew her fears about what people said about her would still persist in her mind.

Chapter *Twelve*

Halloween brought joy to the little town of Baylorsville. Carrie and Sarah's Glenda the witch costumes were a big hit. Jan's confidence in herself as both mom and pastor was growing. She had just gotten into her office on a Tuesday in mid-November when she received a phone call from Linda Williams.

"Pastor Jan," Linda said, her voice shaking. "I took Wanda back to the doctor today. She hasn't responded to the medicine. She's running a low-grade fever again. They want us to take her to Shands Hospital in Gainesville for some tests. I'm really worried. Will you put her on the prayer chain?"

"Of course, Linda. I'll do it right now. Call me when you get the results."

Jan hung up the phone and walked to the window of her office, looking at the swaying pine trees. *Wow, Shands.* The teaching hospital at the University of Florida was three hours away. It was serious if her doctors were referring her there. *Linda and Tom must be frantic.* Jan couldn't imagine how Ben and she would react if Carrie or Sarah were that sick. *What if Wanda's seriously ill?* Could she be the pastor this family needed? She wasn't sure she had the wisdom or the expertise to help a family through this type of crisis. Running her fingers through her hair, she shook her head. *Forgive me, God. Here I am whining and this family's in trouble. Be with the Williams family, especially little*

Wanda. Amen.

Stepping into the office, she asked Betty to start the prayer chain.

The next Tuesday, Jan was in her office preparing for her Thanksgiving Sunday sermon when the phone rang. It was a déjà vu moment when Betty told her Linda wanted to speak to her. Jan knew Linda and little Wanda were at Shands again that morning getting the results from the tests they had done last week. *Oh, God, let this be good news.*

"Hi Linda, how…" Before she could say anything else, Linda's frightened voice cut Jan off.

"Pastor Jan," Linda hiccupped into the phone. "Wanda needs surgery immediately. The doctor says something's wrong with her left kidney. She's being admitted to the hospital right now and will have surgery tomorrow morning. They think she might have… cancer." Linda started crying. "Pastor Jan, Tom and I are so scared."

Jan gasped. "Oh, no, Linda. I'm so sorry." She grabbed for more words but could only say she was sorry over and over. As Linda continued to cry, Jan's mind spun. *Lord, help me. I don't know what else to say.* Finally, Jan began asking questions. "Linda, is Tom with you? Are you going to stay in Gainesville tonight? Is Mary with you?" She hoped the questions would cut through Linda's hysteria.

It worked, as Linda seemed to calm down. After hiccupping a few more times, she spoke again. "I'm staying with Wanda tonight. I can't bear to leave her, but Tom and Mary are leaving to go home in a few minutes. My sister Lucy will meet him at home and stay with Mary, so he'll probably come right back. The surgery time isn't set yet for tomorrow, but could you come?" she asked, crying again.

"Of course, I'll come. I'll be there as soon as I can tomorrow morning. I'll also check on Lucy and Mary tonight." She wished she could hug Linda. "Let me pray with you now and then I'll get the prayer chain started." Jan gripped the phone tighter and prayed, "God, we don't understand what's going on. We're all frightened. Hold on to Linda, Tom, Mary and especially Wanda right now. Be with the doctors and staff. Help them find out what is wrong and, dear God, we pray for healing. Amen." As Jan ended the prayer, she realized she was praying for herself as much as for Linda.

"Thank you, Pastor Jan," Linda sniffed. "This is so unbelievable, but it helps to talk to you…" Linda paused for a moment and Jan could hear a voice in the background. "Pastor Jan, the nurse is here. I think they've got a room for Wanda. I'll see you tomorrow, okay?"

"Of course, Linda. Try to get some sleep tonight. I'll check on Tom when he gets home and have prayer with him. God be with you both, and give Wanda a hug for me." Jan hung up the phone and put her head on her desk.

"Pastor Jan?" Betty whispered from the office door. Jan looked up with tears in her eyes and realized Betty had been listening to her side of the conversation.

She got up and hugged Betty. "Wanda's very sick. The doctors say she might have cancer. The surgeon will remove her left kidney tomorrow morning."

Betty's eyes got wide, and she put both hands over her mouth. Always emotional, Betty burst into tears. Jan held her and they both cried for a few minutes. Grabbing tissues and wiping their eyes, they sat at Betty's desk and planned how to tell the congregation and how to care for this frightened family.

After getting the prayer chain started and lining up meals to take to the family, Jan packed up her sermon material and walked home. She desperately wanted to go to Gainesville to see Linda right then, but she needed to make arrangements for her own family, and she had a church council meeting that night. As she passed the lake, she decided to walk around it a few times. Over the past few months, this small pond had truly become her sanctuary, a safe place where she could think, pray, make decisions, and especially calm her mind, body, and soul. *Lord God, I feel so helpless. I really don't even know what to pray. Of course, I want you to heal Wanda, but cancer is so scary. She's such a special little girl. Surely you will heal her, won't you?* Jan brushed tears away from her eyes. *I trust you, God, but I don't trust me. Will I have the right things to say and the strength to hold this family together? I've never even been with a family with such a sick child. Please be with me. Speak through me. Comfort me so I can comfort them. Amen.*

Leaving the lake, Jan walked home, still reeling from the dreadful news of Wanda's illness, but calmer. The walk around the lake had helped clear her head. She devised a plan to have Ben take the children to school the next day and get an early start for Gainesville.

———————••••••◗••••◄———————

By the time Jan got to Shands at 9:00 the next morning, Wanda was in surgery. Linda, Tom, and Jan waited in uneasy silence in a large waiting room with rows of drab brown chairs. Large plate-glass windows covered one side of the room, but a gloomy, rainy day let in little light. Other people clustered together in tight little groups. A volunteer in a dark blue smock sat at a desk. Every few minutes, the phone would ring and the volunteer would approach one of the groups and hustle them to a private room to receive the news of their loved one's surgery. A few minutes before noon, the phone call was for Linda and Tom. Jan followed as the volunteer showed them to the small room. She and Linda sat at a small table and Tom stood behind them. A few minutes later the surgeon walked in. Jan took one look at him and knew the news was bad. She grasped Linda's hand.

When the doctor glanced at Jan, she said quickly, "I'm Linda and Tom's pastor, Rev. Jan Hendricks."

He nodded to her and looked directly into Linda's eyes.

"Mr. and Mrs. Williams, we removed the kidney, but I'm afraid the cancer has spread. I'm referring Wanda to a cancer specialist for further treatment."

Jan gasped, squeezing Linda's hand. Linda erupted in tears as Tom's face turned red. Jan thought he would hit the doctor. Instead, he punched the top of the table and began pacing around the small room. Jan realized neither one of them could talk so she turned to the doctor.

"Is Wanda all right? How long will she be here?"

The doctor looked quickly at Tom. "She should wake up in about an hour. We'll keep her a week and get started on the treatment. A nurse will come when you can see her." He started to leave but stopped and turned back toward them. "I'm sorry."

Jan's eyes filled with tears. *God, this can't be happening.* She put her arms around Linda as Tom continued pacing. *Lord, help me find the right words to help them.* After holding Linda for a few minutes, Jan realized she had to help them make plans. She glanced at Tom who was propped against the wall with both hands clasped behind his head. She took a deep breath. "Linda, Tom, I'm so sorry. This is such a shock."

Linda looked up at Jan and squeezed her hand. She whispered, "Pastor Jan, I can't lose her." Her body seemed to cave into herself as she bent over and broke into hiccupping sobs.

Tom rushed to gather her in his arms. He was now crying.

The minutes ticked by as they went back into the large room and waited for someone to come and take them to Wanda. Tom alternately paced before the large window and held Linda, who had stopped crying but was shaking. Jan sat beside Linda wishing she could do more for them. The doctor's words "cancer specialist" kept replaying in her head. *God, we can't lose this child. Show me what to do, how to help them. Help this place heal her.* Yet she had seen the look in the doctor's eyes. This was not going to be easy.

After several minutes had passed, she wrapped her arms around both Linda and Tom and mumbled a prayer. "Lord

God, we don't know what to do or to say right now. We love you and we know you love Wanda. Help us through these next few days. Amen." Just as Jan finished her prayer, a nurse appeared and whisked Tom and Linda to see Wanda.

After Wanda had gotten settled in the pediatric ICU, Tom came and got Jan. She flinched when she saw Wanda. Her little body was hooked to several machines and lines ran from her arms. Her body looked so tiny in the big bed. She was pale and her long blond hair was spread around her pillow. Jan had to stop and consciously breathe to keep from gasping out loud. She wanted to gather this child in her arms and whisk her away from this terrible place. Instead, she squeezed Linda's hand and leaned over to kiss Wanda. "We all love you, Wanda. Get well soon." Wanda's eyes flickered open and seemed to recognize Jan. She moved her hand a little and then closed her eyes.

Jan stood up and looked at both Tom and Linda. "Let's pray." They joined hands. "God, we trust you are with Wanda. She's your child and you are already holding her and loving her. We pray for your healing grace to flow through her body. Be with these doctors, nurses, and caregivers. And especially be with Linda and Tom. Watch over them as they wait and help them know how much they are loved. Amen."

Jan left them mid-afternoon and made the long trip back. She needed to hug her daughters.

Four days later, the Sunday before Thanksgiving, Jan walked the short distance to the church. Her mood was heavy with the burden of sharing with the congregation about Wanda's illness. The beauty of the day conflicted with the heaviness of her heart. Deep reds and yellows splashed across the trees against a deep blue sky. Perhaps God was trying to boost her spirits to help her share this sad news.

She entered the quiet sanctuary. It was a cool morning. She smelled the faint odor of burned dust, so she assumed the heat was on. Breathing in the churchy smells of candles, flowers, and stale perfume, she took off her jacket and knelt at the rail. The altar glowed with the decorated cornucopia of bright oranges and yellows of pumpkins, squash, and corn, all grown by members of the congregation.

"Lord," she prayed out loud. "Today is Thanksgiving Sunday. It's a day of celebration, thanking you for all the wonderful gifts you are giving to us, yet it's also the day I must share with these people that an eight-year-old child, a member of this church family, may be dying. Give me strength. Help me say the right words to comfort the Williams family and this church and community. Amen."

Later that morning, Jan followed the choir, singing the Thanksgiving hymn, "Come Thy Thankful People Come." As the choir filed into the loft, she stepped into the pulpit and watched her congregation sing the last few verses of the hymn. Tears filled her eyes as she looked over these people she had grown to love in such a short time. She took a deep breath and motioned them to sit as she said, "Yes, my friends, we are gathering as a thankful people. The harvest is in and we are mindful of all that God has given us. But on this day on which we express our thanks to God, we also need to pray for the Williams family."

She gazed at her congregation. The Williams family was in Gainesville, but many of their friends were in the sanctuary. Ben and the girls were in their customary front pew. Betty, sitting in the second row, was already sobbing. Mike and Susan Rollins and their four precious boys were there. Madge, Sadie, and Mona were sitting in the back, alongside the Cullens family and their two children. Jan paused, gazing at these people. This was the family of First Church, people who would be there through thick and thin, the good times and the hard times. She took another deep breath and began.

"Many of you are aware little Wanda Williams has been sick for the past few months. Tests were taken at Shands Children's

Hospital in Gainesville last week, and a very rare form of kidney cancer was diagnosed. Thank you for praying for her and her family when she went through surgery, but the outcome doesn't look good and the Williams family is asking for earnest prayer as she begins treatment." Jan stopped as she took another deep breath, trying to keep from crying, and looked at her congregation. *Lord, be with me.*

She swallowed and continued, "We don't know when she or they will be home. Tom's job has given him time off and the family is staying at the Ronald McDonald house near Shands. I'm going weekly to see them, but they need your prayers. So, let's start our Thanksgiving service with a prayer for this family."

Amidst continuing sobs, Jan struggled through the rest of the service.

Chapter Thirteen

Wanda came home from the hospital the first week in December. The day after she returned, Jan picked up Carrie early from the after-school program and visited the Williams. They brought a pan of freshly baked banana bread. This would be a tough visit and Jan hoped she could bring some sense of peace to the family.

Wanda was sitting cross-legged on their worn couch with a brightly colored afghan wrapped around her. The surgery had left her pale with sunken eyes. Jan's heart tore as she watched Carrie stop and absorb the reality that her best friend looked very different. Carrie's eyes widened, but at Wanda's bright smile, she bounded over to her, hugging her fiercely. She placed the small Christmas bear she had insisted on buying when they were in the grocery store in Wanda's lap. Wanda squealed, hugging the bear to her chest, and they began the excited chatter that only eight-year-olds could do. Jan followed Linda into the kitchen.

"She seems to have tolerated the surgery," Linda said as she poured them glasses of sweet iced tea. "But she's too weak to begin the chemo treatments. They hope to start them the first week of the New Year." Linda began to cry and sat in one of the vinyl kitchen chairs." At least we'll have her home for Christmas."

Jan reached for some tissues on the counter and gave them to Linda. She couldn't imagine Linda's pain. Jan sat in a chair beside Linda and put an arm around her shoulder.

After a few minutes, Linda sniffed and blew her nose. "I'm sorry." She swiped at her eyes as she glanced into the den where the girls were talking about the dolls each wanted for Christmas. "I'm crying all the time."

Jan handed her another tissue. "Don't be sorry. You have every right to cry." *I don't think I would ever stop crying.*

Linda wiped her eyes. "This is so hard." She got up and paced around the cramped kitchen. "Tom's job has given him two extra weeks off, so he can be with us when Wanda goes back to Shands for the therapy, but when he's used that, he won't get paid. So, he'll have to stay in town and work and won't be able to come with us."

Linda sat again, taking a long sip of her tea. She set the glass down, rested her elbow on the table, and rubbed her head. "Tom seems so strong, but I know he's hurting." Jan listened, knowing Linda needed to talk.

Shaking her head, Linda continued, "And Mary's so confused." She looked right into Jan's eyes. "How do you tell your five-year-old that her sister may die?" Linda hiccupped and grabbed more tissue.

Jan's eyes were tearing now. *Lord, give me the right words.* Linda was searching for ways to make sense of this tragedy. And she depended on Jan to help. Jan needed to draw deep into her skills as a pastor and her own faith to help this struggling family. She breathed deeply, grabbed both of Linda's hands and looked deep into her eyes.

"Linda, I'm so sorry you're going through this. I wish we could make this go away. I don't have the answers, but God does. And I know God is holding Wanda and all of you in his hands. He will get you through this."

Jan stood up, reached into her purse, and handed her friend an envelope. "The church council wants you to have this. We know Wanda's illness has taken a toll on your finances. We can't do much, but we can help with your bills and pray for you."

Linda hugged Jan. "Thanks. This'll really help, especially with travel expenses." She opened the envelope and gasped. Her eyes got wide as she saw the thousand-dollar check inside.

"Oh, Pastor Jan, this is too much."

Jan smiled as she hugged her again. "Your church and this town love you very much. We can't take away Wanda's illness, but we can do this."

Tom appeared with Mary in tow. They had been to the pharmacy and grocery shopping. He came into the kitchen putting the grocery bags on the counter. "Hey Pastor Jan," he said, coming over and kissing his wife's forehead. "Thanks for coming." He gave Mary a little pat on the head as she smiled at Jan and bounded into the other room to join Wanda and Carrie.

"Got two of her medicines. The other one they had to order from Tallahassee. Should be in after six tonight." He began unloading the groceries.

Tom looked tired. He worked long hours at the Department of Transportation and obviously had worked today. He probably had gotten little sleep in the hospital. In the several months Jan knew him, she had sensed a deep pride in him. He barely had a high school education but seemed focused and steady with his job. He loved his wife and little girls. Jan didn't know how he would handle having to depend on people to help him. He regularly attended church, but Jan was unsure of the depth of his faith. Wanda's illness would test everything for this young family. She wasn't sure how Tom would react to the check. She hoped the monetary gift would show how much the town loved him and his family.

"Tom, we're so glad you and the girls are home," Jan said getting up. "Thanks for the tea, Linda. Can we gather in the living room for prayer before Carrie and I go?"

As they held hands, Jan tried to keep from crying. She tightly held Carrie's hand and prayed, "Holy God, we love you and know you love us. Hold this family in your loving arms as they go through this time of uncertainty. Enter Wanda's body and let your healing love flow through her as she battles this illness. Give Linda and Tom and Mary your strength as they travel with Wanda through this. And be with the doctors and caretakers as they claim your direction with her treatment. In the name of Jesus, we pray. Amen."

Jan took Carrie's hand as they walked home. An overcast sky made the late afternoon darker than normal. The air was turning colder and Jan pulled her sweater a little closer. She hoped she had given the Williamses some sense of hope that she and the church community were supporting them. Suddenly, she realized that Carrie was quiet, too quiet. She looked down to see her crying.

Jan knelt and wiped the tears away from her face. "Sweetheart, what's wrong?"

"Mom, some kids at school say Wanda will die," she whispered. "I don't want her to die. Do you think she will?"

Jan hugged her daughter. *O God, how do I do this? How do I tell my little girl that, yes, her best friend might die? Please guide me.*

Hugging Carrie, Jan wiped at her own eyes. "We don't know if Wanda will die. She has a terrible disease and the doctors are doing everything they can for her."

"But Jesus will make her better, won't he, Mama?"

Jan's heart broke. She knelt and hugged her daughter. "We all pray Jesus will make her better, sweetie."

Jan held Carrie for several seconds, praying God would give her the right words for Carrie. She needed to tell Carrie how ill Wanda was, and yet to do so would chip away Carrie's innocence.

With tears running down Jan's face, she rose, took Carrie's hand, and headed home.

<hr />

"Let's put the decorations on our tree tonight," Jan said as they finished supper. She had told Ben about Carrie's questions about Wanda's illness, and they had decided to be honest with the girls with what might happen to Wanda. Jan hoped she and Ben would somehow be able to comfort their little girl.

They adjourned to the living room where, amidst hoots and laughter, the girls attacked the boxes of Christmas decorations, which were stacked near the artificial tree Ben had put up earlier that afternoon.

Jan picked up a small silver angel given to her by an elderly woman a few years ago. It was one of her favorites and the first Christmas tree decoration they put on the tree each year.

"Carrie, where should we put our special angel this year?"

Carrie studied the tree and took the angel from Jan. "We need to put her at the top where she can protect the other decorations."

"Sounds like a plan," Ben said. He lifted Carrie up and she placed it at the top of the tree. Jan glanced at Ben as he set Carrie down on the floor. He nodded and sat on the couch. Jan sighed and put her arm around Carrie.

"Carrie, remember when you asked me about Wanda this afternoon?"

Carrie looked at Jan and nodded, curling her small body into Jan's embrace.

Jan sighed, swallowed, and gazed into Carrie's eyes. "I want you to know, Carrie, God will take care of Wanda. He loves her very much, but sometimes God takes care of people in ways we don't always understand."

Carrie's little face scrunched up. Sarah stopped putting ornaments on the tree and climbed on Ben's lap, listening to her mother. Jan looked at her two little girls, caught Ben's eye, and continued.

"And sometimes, yes, that means that our bodies won't get well. But that doesn't mean God doesn't love us. In fact, that means God loves us so much more. God reaches into our lives and the lives of those around us and wraps us in lots and lots of love."

"But I don't want God to wrap me in lots of love." Carrie was crying now. "I want God to make Wanda well. My Sunday school teacher said Jesus once healed a little girl. Why can't Jesus heal Wanda?"

Jan sat beside Ben and pulled Carrie into her lap. *How do I have a theological discussion with a child?* "I know, sweetheart. Jesus did heal that little girl. But sometimes Jesus heals us in different ways."

"Well, I don't understand why Jesus can't heal Wanda. It's not fair she's sick. And it's Christmas time and everything's supposed to be fun and happy." Carrie jerked from Jan's lap and rummaged through the Christmas bulbs. She picked up a small silver bell and hung it on the tree.

Jan got up, knelt beside Carrie, and placed her hand on Carrie's shoulder. "We all want Wanda to get well. And it's not fair she's sick. But God is still with her and her family."

Carrie turned and looked at Jan. "Well, I believe that Jesus will fix Wanda." That said, Carrie turned back around and rummaging in the box of decorations, found another angel and placed it on the tree.

Jan looked over at Ben. He was rubbing Sarah's back with tears in his eyes. Jan watched Carrie go back and forth to the box of decorations, almost defiantly picking each one out and placing it on the tree. *God, help my baby.*

They spent another half hour decorating the tree. Carrie remained subdued, and Sarah bounced back and forth, putting most of her decorations on the bottom of the tree, but the gaiety had gone out of the evening for Jan. By the time they finally turned the lights on the tree, with both girls clapping their hands over the colorful lights, Jan yearned for sleep.

After putting the girls to bed, Jan lay on the bed as Ben came out of the bathroom.

"You okay?" he asked, climbing in beside her.

"Yeah, I guess so." She rolled over and sat up against the pillow, running her hand through her hair. "Do you think Carrie understands what's happening? I believe in miracles and I pray with everything I've got that God will heal Wanda from this awful disease. But I'm afraid that's not going to happen. She's so sick and so frail. How will Carrie take this? What if she's so traumatized by Wanda's illness and death that she loses her faith?"

Jan grabbed a tissue and swiped at her eyes as they filled with tears. She threw the damp tissue on the nightstand. "I'm ashamed that Carrie's fears are on my mind right now and not on what Tom and Linda are going through." She pounded the pillow. "Some pastor I am." She flung the covers off, jumped up, and paced the bedroom. "I'm so angry, and so frustrated. Carrie's right. It's not fair that Wanda's so sick. I don't understand why this child even got this horrible disease. I question what God is doing, too." After pacing for a few minutes, she sat on the bed, covering her eyes with her hands.

"You know, there're no clear answers for this," Ben said, pulling Jan's hands off her tear-streaked face. "But I believe God will give you what you need to get the Williams family and the church through this crisis." He pushed tear-streaked hair out of Jan's eyes. "And of course, you're going to worry about how Carrie reacts to this. You're her mom. But you said some powerful things to her tonight. All you can be is honest with her and love her. She'll get through this. We all will."

"I hope so." Settling back in the bed, Jan wiped her eyes and blew her nose. Ben pulled the covers over them as Jan turned out the lights. *God, I hope so. Please be with my little Carrie.*

The next morning, Jan woke to Carrie's gentle kiss on her cheek. She opened her eyes and sat up.

"Hi, sweetheart. What's wrong?"

Carrie looked puzzled. She petted her mom's face, something she'd been doing since she was a baby.

"Mom, I had a dream about Wanda. She was alone and

scared and then she died. I was upset and crying, but then I saw Jesus holding her, and she wasn't hurting anymore. And I had a happy heart."

Carrie stopped for a minute and then said, "Do you think that's how it'll be for her in heaven, that she'll not be afraid and alone?"

Jan's heart lurched. *Out of the mouths of babies, sweet Jesus.* "Yes, Carrie, I think that's how she'll feel in heaven." Jan put her arms around Carrie as Ben sat up and pulled her into bed with them, hugging her too.

Chapter Fourteen

Jan had been looking forward to celebrating Christmas in Baylorsville. The anticipation of this small-town holiday promised to be heartwarming. However, the dark cloud surrounding Wanda's illness threatened Jan's joy about the season. She was afraid it was affecting Carrie, too. Despite the dream Carrie had had about Wanda being safe in Jesus' arms, her daughter had been quiet and moody.

But it was impossible not to be caught up in the holiday spirit. The whole town began decorating the Sunday after Thanksgiving. The church had wreaths on their doors and red ribbons on the pews. Most of the downtown businesses glowed with the bright reds and greens of the season. Baylorsville was ready for Christmas.

The highlight of the season was the annual parade, always held the second Saturday night of December. The schools, scout troops, civic groups, and churches all had their special floats. First Church had been planning their float for months. They were using the theme "The Little Drummer Boy," and the children were characters in the nativity scene. Carrie and Sarah, along with the other children of the church, spent several chaotic afternoons working on their float.

On the evening of the parade, Ben, Jan, and the girls walked to where the floats were being staged. Jan paid special atten-

tion to Carrie. Normally she would have been running ahead
of them, with Sarah right behind. But it was Sarah, dressed as
an angel, who was in the lead, trying to catch up with the other children. Carrie was quiet and sticking right beside Jan and
Ben. Before they reached the float, Carrie looked up at Jan.

"Wanda was supposed to be a shepherd. I'm sad she won't
get to ride on the float."

Jan knelt in front of her daughter. "I know, Carrie. I'm sad
Wanda can't be in the parade, too. But the doctor wants her to
stay away from crowds."

"Well, I guess that makes sense." Carrie frowned. "But I'm
still sad for her. It's just not fair she's sick for Christmas." Carrie shrugged her shoulders and climbed on the float. She was
playing the role of Mary, the mother of Jesus. Jan watched her
daughter settle beside the manger, arranging her bulky robe
over the bale of hay. Carrie picked up the doll representing the
baby Jesus and cradled it in her arms. Jan looked away so Carrie wouldn't see her tears. How was she going to get through
this season as a pastor, much less a mom?

As if reading her mind, Ben squeezed her hand. Jan looked
up at him.

"It'll be okay."

"I hope so," she said, and before she had time to say anything else, Sarah grabbed her hand.

"Mama, look." Sarah pointed to the blinking red, green and
blue lights draped across Main Street, which held colored wire
frames of Christmas characters. "Santa Claus and his reindeer
are on the street lights."

Picking Sarah up, Ben laughed. He deposited her in the float
alongside a tow-headed boy dressed as the drummer boy,
who was beating on the drum. Several other children from the
church were already there, in the costumes of shepherds, wise
men, and angels. The temperature had dropped again, and the
children looked more like padded snowmen than the Nativity
scene characters. Sarah scrambled up on top of the bale of hay

lining the side and immediately bumped into the wall of the stable, knocking her angel wings off.

"Daddy, look behind us! It's, it's Santa Claus!" Sarah stood, pointing to the last vehicle in the parade, which indeed held the red-coated Santa.

Ben climbed up beside her and pulled her to the center of the float, straightening her wings.

"I see him Sarah, but you've got to stay on the inside of the hay if you're going to ride." He helped another child in a shepherd costume climb onto the float and guided both children to the wooden stable. "Now, stay there."

Jan watched him fiddle with the tape recorder and turn on the music. He had worked hard making a loop of "The Little Drummer Boy" song so it would play along the mile-long parade route. He jumped off the float and joined Jan and the other parents who would walk beside it, keeping a careful eye on the children. Jan took his hand.

"Sarah is so excited. I don't think she'll stay inside that stable," Jan said, laughing.

"Don't think so either, but the others are standing, too," Ben said. He shouted once more to Sarah to sit.

A woman's voice called out Jan's name, and she glanced into the crowd. Betty Smith was wildly clapping and shouting at the children on the float.

"Yay, First Church, you look great!" she called. Several other church members standing beside her echoed the phrase. "You're the best float in the parade."

Though the children were told to be still, in their excitement they still waved to the crowd. Jan looked at the joyful children and then at the crowds lining the parade route. The lights, the laughter, the excitement called to her. Christmas was a special time in Baylorsville.

Even with Wanda's illness, the hope and joy of Christmas were prevailing. A sense of peace came over her. Yes, it would be hard, very hard, to embrace the pain the Williamses and this community would feel at Wanda's impending death. And yes, Jan knew deep in her heart, even with the faithful prayers of this community, Wanda would soon die. It would be a terrible time for everyone. And Jan would feel this pain deeply, but life would go on. Jan glanced at the crowd again and smiled. *Thanks, God. I know you'll get us through this.*

The high school band broke into "Jingle Bells," and the parade began. Ben grabbed her hand, and they walked beside the float. Jan took a deep breath. Even in the midst of pain, and perhaps because of pain, Christmas was coming.

Chapter Fifteen

Christmas Eve morning, Jan was in her office putting the final touches on her message for that night's service, when the outside door opened. She heard Betty's startled greeting.

"Why, hi, John. We haven't seen you for a while. How've you been?"

Jan's heart raced. *Now what?* She had not seen John since he had resigned from the treasurer's position and stalked out of her office at the end of August. She had seen Martha at the small grocery store in town a few weeks ago and said hello to her, but Martha had just nodded and hurried out the store. Jan figured John was still angry, and she didn't have time for a confrontation this morning.

She braced herself as Betty entered her office doorway with John in tow.

"John, it's good to see you. Merry Christmas," Jan said as John pushed his way past Betty into her tiny study. Martha was not with him. He shut the door in Betty's face. Jan stood to greet him and put out her hand, but he waved it off. His face was flushed. *Oh, Lord.*

"Please sit," she said gesturing toward the chair in front of her desk. He ignored the invitation to sit, so Jan remained standing.

"I understand you've given the Williams family money from

the church," John began.

Jan's cheeks burned. "Where did you hear this?" Jan asked, her tone icy. "It's none of your business."

"Of course, it's my business!" He slammed his hand on Jan's desk, knocking off a book. "This is my church. We don't have the money to throw around on people like the Williamses!"

"Wait just a minute, John." She picked up the book that John had knocked off and slammed it back on her desk. "First, the money the church gave to the Williams family comes from my discretionary fund, which our mission committee controls.

"Second, most of the money the church gave them was given to me by folks who earmarked it for the Williams family. Under church law that money has to go to them." Jan had gotten right into John's face. She clenched her fists but kept them by her side.

"And third, you have no right to enter this discussion. You haven't attended this church in several months, and you gave up your position as treasurer." Jan's heart was beating twice its normal rate, and she was breathing hard.

"Now, I'm going to ask you to leave." She walked around him, and opened the door, standing to the side as she motioned him out with her hand. "You're too angry right now. We'll talk later."

Betty was standing at the door, her mouth open. John stomped past her.

"This isn't over," he growled, slamming the door.

Jan's hands were shaking. She looked up at Betty and tears slid down her cheeks. "That man makes me so angry. All my training goes out the window when he comes through that door."

Betty surprised Jan by clapping and giving her a big hug. "Well, I think you handled it just right. Sorry, I couldn't help but overhear. He was pretty loud. But he needed to hear what you said. What a piece of work he is. I can't believe he bothered you on Christmas Eve."

"Yeah, not good timing, I wonder who told him about the gift and what he's spreading around the town. I would hate for the Williams family to hear this."Jan glanced out the window as John's big truck screeched out of the parking lot. "Linda and Tom are dealing with enough, and Tom didn't want to even take the money." Jan pushed her hair behind her ears and massaged her temples. She had a lot to do before that evening. Presents still needed to be wrapped and packing still needed to be done for their trip to Clearwater Christmas afternoon. She also wanted to make a quick trip to see Wes Atkins, one of her shut-ins who had no family. It was 10:30, and she wanted to be home by 2:00.

Betty shuffled back to her desk and continued folding the Christmas Eve bulletins. She called through to Jan's office. "Well, I wouldn't worry what John is saying. You know me, I listen to the town gossip. And they like you, Pastor Jan. You're getting a wonderful reputation of loving the people here and that's all they want. John just wants his own way. I was in the drug store the other day and saw John talking to Jerry, the pharmacist. Jerry knows John is a member here and I overheard Jerry asking him how the church is dealing with the Williams' troubles. Well, John started talking about how the church is going downhill because of, 'scuse me, Pastor Jan, 'that woman,' and Jerry defended you. Said he heard you were great. I was right proud of the way he talked."

Jan half-smiled.

Betty finished the bulletins and rapped them sharply against the desk, forming a neat stack. "Pastor Jan, people aren't paying John much mind."

Jan plopped down in the hard-back chair next to Betty's desk. "Do you know what's going on with him? Has he always been this, uh, disagreeable?"

"Well, I don't rightly know too much about him and Martha. But I have always wondered if something happened in their past to make them move here." Betty leaned back in her desk chair, scrunching up her face. "They've been here maybe ten years. They came from somewhere up north and settled in along the lake near the Georgia border. I think John worked in a bank and Martha just kept house."

"They must have been in their early fifties when they came to town," Jan said."I know they're in their sixties now. Did he work when they got here?"

Betty shook her head. "Nope. He came to church and when we found out he'd been in banking, we asked him to be the trea-surer and he said yes. Been the treasurer ever since until he quit."

Jan winced at that. They still had not found a permanent treasurer. Betty was paying the bills for now, and they had three people signing the checks, but they needed a treasurer. Jan hoped they could find one by the beginning of the year.

"Do they have children?"

"Don't think so," Betty said, standing and stretching her bulky frame. She refilled her coffee, raising the cup in the air to see if Jan wanted more. At Jan's shake of her head, she contin-ued. "In fact, I don't think they have any other family. At least none they've mentioned. They're both really private people."

"What about Martha? She seems so timid. Has she ever worked?"

"I don't know. She always seems so sad, though, and kind of overshadowed by John. She hardly says a word." Betty looked at Jan. "I've always felt sorry for her."

"Yeah, I'm feeling that way, too." Jan stood. "Well, I'm not getting any more done here this morning. I'll go check on Wes and go home to get ready for tonight." She smiled at Betty. "Don't stay too long. It is, after all, Christmas Eve."

"Oh, I plan to leave by noon. I just want to finish up the bul-letin for next week's service. If I don't get a chance to speak to you tonight, have a wonderful trip and a great time with your family. And don't worry about the church, especially John. He'll come around."

Jan went back into her office and packed up her notes. She

gave Betty a hug, left the office and walked toward home. She would get her car and drive to visit Wes. But on nearing the small lake, she decided to calm her soul by walking around it. The mid-December morning had been cold when she left the house earlier, but as many of the winter days in North Florida, it was now perfect weather to walk. She gazed at the water, which was becoming very special to her. Because it was mid-morning, no one was around. Baylorsville was proud of this lake and had made the surrounding ground nice. The half-mile mulched path made it easy to walk. Pine trees, decades-old oak trees, and carefully tended grass provided a natural environment for birds and other wildlife. It had become Jan's sanctuary, and she breathed in the cool air. The birds shared a classic symphony as she walked on the path.

God, I'm so tired of these confrontations with John. Why did he come today of all days? Every time I see him, I lose confidence in myself. I don't like the way he saps my strength and self-worth.

Rounding the farthest corner of the lake, a splash caught her attention, and she stopped. Tall wispy grass blocked her view of this part of the lake and she moved closer to get a better look. The trees, though losing some leaves, were still covered with the long, tangled, Spanish tree moss, and she pushed it aside to see better. Another splash drew her attention to an otter frolicking in the water. It flipped back and forth in the shallow water, but soon disappeared. She walked closer to the water's edge and jumped back as it popped up right in front of her as if to say, "Won't you come and play with me?" Jan laughed. The antics of the otter comforted her. It reminded her to not take things so seriously. It wasn't up to her to make John Tully respect her. She just needed to be faithful to God and try to love these people to the best of her ability. Continuing her walk, she smiled. *Thanks, God, for this Christmas miracle. I guess you can speak even through an otter.*

Feeling rejuvenated from the lake encounter with the otter and having accomplished her "to do" list, Jan enjoyed their family Christmas Eve dinner and even rested. She, Ben, and the girls walked to the church that evening. Carrie and Sarah wore matching red velvet Christmas dresses with white tights and black patent leather shoes. In their excitement, the girls skipped, twirled, and danced down the street, as only children on Christmas Eve could do.

Ben escorted the girls into the sanctuary where they had one more choir practice, while Jan headed into her office. She sat behind her desk and studied her short message. The service consisted of carols, special music from the choirs and soloists, and the candle lighting ceremony, so she didn't want to preach long. Her heart raced as she thought how important this first Christmas Eve service was. *Dear God, I love this service. Help it go well.* She glanced at her robe, which was hanging from a hook on her closet door, and her heart rate slowed when she saw the white Christmas stole hanging on the robe. The handcrafted linen stole with a light blue angel cross-stitched on one side and a wooden manger with the Christ child stitched on the other side had been a going-away gift from a beloved former church member, Grace Thomas. Grace had an inordinate sense for ministry and was Jan's friend, mentor, and champion. She put the robe on, gently fingered the stole, and strode confidently to the sanctuary. *Grace, this is for you.*

The service went well. As the congregation sang *Silent Night,* and they lifted their lit candles, Jan's heart warmed. *Holy God, thank you for this service, for the six months I have been here. I have faced battles and actually won some of them. There have been great times and some bad times. It hasn't always been easy, but it has been fulfilling.*

This was her congregation. A mixture of peace and relief descended on her at the close of the service. The tirade John Tully caused that morning melted away as Jan absorbed the ambiance of the service. All was well on this blessed Holy Night.

Chapter Sixteen

"Mom, Dad, get up, it's Christmas, " Carrie yelled, bounding into the bedroom. She pulled Jan out of bed.

Thus began the six a.m. rush of opening presents—dolls, books and crayons for the girls—and the traditional pancake breakfast for the Hendricks family. It was a fun, hectic morning, but right before their eleven a.m. departure for their Christmas week trip to see the grandparents, Jan found Carrie curled up on the couch in the den clutching her new doll and crying.

"Sweetheart, what's wrong?" Jan asked, setting down the toiletry bag she was carrying and pulling Carrie into a hug. "You're not supposed to be upset on Christmas day."

"But, Mom," Carrie whispered, "is it okay for me to be happy when Wanda's so sick?"

The joy drained from the room. What could Jan say to make Carrie feel better? She rubbed Carrie's back as Ben came into the room carrying a suitcase, with Sarah trailing after him. Jan looked up at him as he raised his eyebrows. She motioned for him to sit down beside Carrie.

Jan sighed deeply, searching for the right words to comfort her child. "Carrie," she finally said. "Do you remember the dream you had the other day?"

Carrie snuggled closer to her mother and nodded.

"Wanda was happy in the dream, wasn't she?"

Carrie nodded again, as Sarah snuggled in between Jan and Ben.

"Well," Jan continued as she looked at Ben, who gave her a slight nod. "I believe Jesus is telling you that it's okay for you to be happy because Jesus is going to help Wanda be happy." Jan hoped she was saying the right words to help both her daughters.

Carrie sat up and scrunched her face. She finally smiled and looked at Jan. "Yeah, I guess Jesus does want me to be happy on Christmas morning." She hugged her mom.

Ben stood, pulling Carrie up with him as he wrapped her in a hug. "I'm sure Wanda and Mary are having a wonderful Christmas morning," he said. He motioned for Jan to rise, too. "We'd better get going, or we'll miss Christmas dinner with your grandparents."

As Carrie and Sarah grabbed their dolls and followed Ben to the car, Jan closed her eyes for a moment. *Thanks for those words, God.* She hoped God would continue to give her the words to help not only her children, but the church, too, as Wanda got sicker.

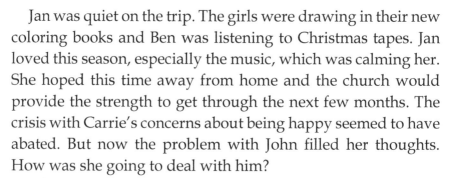

Jan was quiet on the trip. The girls were drawing in their new coloring books and Ben was listening to Christmas tapes. Jan loved this season, especially the music, which was calming her. She hoped this time away from home and the church would provide the strength to get through the next few months. The crisis with Carrie's concerns about being happy seemed to have abated. But now the problem with John filled her thoughts. How was she going to deal with him?

They arrived in Clearwater in time for the Christmas dinner Jan's parents, Helen and Bill, had prepared. Jan and Ben were both only children and Ben's parents had died in a car accident during his junior year in college, so the gathering around the table was few, but filled with laughter and love. Ben considered Jan's parents his, too. After they unwrapped their gifts, and the girls were busy dressing their dolls in the new clothes, Jan and Ben sat in the kitchen with her parents. They chatted about the Christmas Eve service and caught up on the news from the church. Helen asked about little Wanda and Jan explained how ill Wanda was, and the fear she would not live. The conversation turned to Jan's problems with John Tully. Jan regularly talked with her parents about the troubles with John. Bill looked at Jan. "What're you going to do about John?"

Ben put his arm around Jan as she answered, "I'm not sure. I need to find out what's wrong. He's a grumpy man, but from what I gather in talking with other people, he's not usually mean. I don't understand why he's upset with the money we gave the Williams family."

Helen added, "Well, I'm not sure you should interact with him at all. Maybe you should tell your secretary not to let him in your office anymore."

Jan leaned her head against the couch. Her mom's words were tempting. She wanted to talk with her mom more and get her advice, but she knew the delicate situation with John was not something her mom would understand. "Can't do that, Mom. He's a member of the church."

"Well, I worry…"

"You know what, Mom? I'm seeing my friend Sandy this week. You remember her? She's one of the chaplains at Tampa General Hospital. I plan to pick her brain about a lot of things, but especially John. Bet she can give me some advice."

Helen started to respond, but Bill jumped up. "Hey, Ben, let's take the dog for a walk."

Jan used the interruption to suggest bedtime for the girls. With a grateful glance to her dad, she called to the girls in the living room and headed down the hall toward the bathroom. Helen followed. Jan didn't want to worry her mom, nor did she want to argue with her. She would just get Helen involved in the bedtime rituals of her grandchildren and hope her mom forgot about the conversation.

Two days later Jan entered a small deli near Tampa General Hospital on Davis Island near downtown Tampa. Sandy, a petite woman with short, bright red hair and a heart-shaped, freckled face, was already sitting in a back booth. Sandy was wearing a dark clergy shirt with a clerical collar. She jumped up as Jan arrived.

"Oh, I have missed you so much," Jan said, embracing her.

"Me, too!" Sandy said.

They caught up with each other, sharing the highlights of the last few months. Though they talked often on the phone, it didn't replace face-to-face girl time.

As they ate, Sandy forked a piece of hard-boiled egg and looked at Jan. "Ok, how are you doing? When you called two weeks ago, you said you needed to talk about something. So…"

Jan pushed her salad around her plate. "Well, things are getting hard. As I shared with you the other week, the little girl, Wanda, is not doing well. She's home, but I'm not sure she will get better." Jan stopped and swiped at a tear. "Sorry," she said, glancing up at Sandy. "But responding to Wanda's illness and her family's pain is so hard. How do you do it, being around dying people all the time?"

Sandy reached out and took Jan's hand. "Jan, most of the people I come into contact with I either don't know or have just met. I can be much more clinical when I minister to them. But you have interacted with this family, and your daughter is this little girl's best friend. It's much more difficult for you to be objective. In fact, you can't be, you shouldn't be." Sandy dropped Jan's hand and took a sip of water. "I'm so sorry, but this might be the very reason you're at this church right now." She smiled at Jan. "Your gift of compassion is what your church needs.

God will get you through this. And I'm praying hard for you."

Jan pushed a strand of hair behind her ear. "Thanks, Sandy. I pray for you, too."

They ate in silence for a few minutes.

"Hey," Sandy said, spearing a carrot with her fork, "what's going on with your nemesis, John?" Jan had kept Sandy up to date on the problems she was having with him.

Jan made a face. "Oh, let me tell you what he did Christmas Eve morning." She pushed her uneaten salad away, leaned her elbows on the table, and shared what had happened.

Sandy's mouth dropped open. "What did you do?" She, too, pushed her salad away, but hers was mostly eaten.

Jan chuckled. "I was actually kind of proud of myself. I told him the money came from different people in the congregation, that this wasn't his business, and asked him to leave. Oh, and I also wished him Merry Christmas."

Sandy laughed. "Good for you. Did he leave?"

"Yep, and Betty, who heard everything because John was being so loud, applauded me when he left. She told me she was proud of me for standing up to him."

"Good for her. I'd like to meet Betty one day. She sounds like a great person."

"She is and she's so supportive of the church and me."

Jan got quiet and Sandy raised her eyebrows. "What else?"

"Well, even though I was mad as heck, Betty and I talked about him after he left. I asked her why he was so grumpy. And she wondered if something in his past made him the way he is." Jan ran her fingers through her hair. "This may sound strange, but I feel sorry for him. And I don't know what to do about that."

Sandy laughed again. "Sounds like some of that stuff we learned in our clinical pastoral class in seminary rubbed off on you. You sound like a pastor."

"How's that?"

"Well, you're mad at him and yet you still want to minister

to him. That's the pastor in you coming out."

"Maybe. What should I do?"

"Pray, pray, pray, and then talk to him."

"Talk to him? But I've tried and he won't listen. It'll take a miracle for that to happen."

"You're in the business of miracles." As Jan laughed, Sandy looked at her watch.

"Well, I'm not on vacation anymore, and I need to get back to the hospital."

Outside the deli, they hugged and promised to keep in touch.

Jan slowly walked to her car. *Talk to John?* She thought about that. John didn't talk to her; he yelled at her. But she needed to be his pastor, even if he didn't want it. She wondered again what was going on with him.

A few days later, they left for home. Jan's time away with her family had fed her soul. Feeling rejuvenated and spiritually refreshed, she decided to take Sandy's advice and find a way to talk to the Tullys.

January arrived dark and dreary. Everyone was talking about the strange weather. Even though North Florida got cold during January and February, rarely did they see several days in a row without sunshine. It was the end of January and Jan was in her study working on her Sunday sermon. Betty was in the front office, complaining about the weather, when the phone rang.

"Pastor Jan, it's Linda Williams," Betty called through the open study door.

Jan picked up the extension in her office and winced. Linda was crying.

"Pastor Jan," Linda cried, "Wanda is worse. We're taking her back to Gainesville today. They will do more treatment on her. Could you get the prayer chain going?"

"Of course, Linda, do you want me to come?"

"Oh, yes. Please come soon. I'm waiting for Tom and we'll leave as soon as he gets here."

"I'll be right there." Even as Jan was putting the phone down, Betty had already reached for the phone on her desk to start the prayer chain. Jan's heart pounded as she rushed to the Williams' home. *I'm not ready for this. None of us are. Be with this family. Be with me.*

Jan followed Linda and Tom to Gainesville and waited with them while the hospital admitted Wanda. They had picked up Mary from school and the little girl was curled in her father's lap. Jan knelt beside her.

Mary said with the honesty of a five-year-old, "Wanda's very sick, Pastor Jan. She needs lots of prayers."

"Yes, Mary, she is sick, but all of us are praying for her." Jan breathed deeply to keep from crying. She looked into Tom's eyes and found them hard and angry. Jan wished she could take this pain away from them but knew she couldn't. She prayed silently for guidance. They sat for several minutes until a nurse came and took them to Wanda. Linda asked Jan if she could stay with Mary.

"Absolutely, we'll go to the play room. Come get us when you can." Jan stood and took Mary's hand as Linda and Tom followed the nurse. Her heart broke as she watched them slowly walk hand-in-hand to their daughter's room.

Two hours later, Jan headed for home. She regretted leaving this broken family but needed to get back to her own. Jan's eyes filled as she remembered little Mary curled in bed with a pale and silent Wanda. Mary had been patting Wanda's head, telling her she loved her.

Wanda stayed in the hospital for two weeks while they did more therapy. Jan visited them at least twice a week, but at the end of the second week, the doctors sent Wanda home to die.

Chapter Seventeen

On Valentine's Day, Carrie came into the kitchen dressed and ready for school. She slid into her seat.

"Hi, honey, Happy Valentine's Day!" Jan said.

When Carrie didn't respond, Jan glanced at her. Carrie was staring into her cereal bowl.

"What's wrong, sweetheart? You're supposed to be happy on this special day."

Carrie looked up at her mother. "Well, today we give out our cards, and I've got one for Wanda, but she won't be at school. I'm sad. She won't get them from her friends."

Jan bent down and planted a kiss on Carrie's head. *Why God, why does this poor innocent child have to die and why do these children, my children, have to go through a death of a friend?*

A wave of frustration and anger swept over her. But Jan was the pastor here. She needed to keep control of her feelings. The Williams family, the congregation, the town, and her family depended on her to be strong.

She took a deep breath and responded, "Well, Carrie, you can gather her cards and take them to her after school."

Carrie stopped eating for a minute. She scrunched her forehead and pressed her lips together. "Yes, that'll work, I'll take them to her. That'll make her feel better." She continued with her breakfast.

Jan studied her daughter for a few minutes, hoping Carrie would find some comfort in the plan. But Sarah's arriving and demanding her breakfast turned her attention away from Carrie. *Please help her, God.*

Ben came bounding into the kitchen. "Bye all," he said. "Happy Valentine's Day. Remember, you're coming to Tallahassee late this afternoon to meet me for dinner to celebrate. I'll see you later." He kissed both girls on the tops of their heads and pecked Jan's cheek. He picked up a piece of toast and a large cup of coffee and headed toward the carport.

Jan smiled as she sat at the table and ate her bagel. Carrie was busy telling Sarah how much fun they would have at school with the valentine parties. She looked at Carrie and marveled at how quickly her child rebounded.

The quick healing of youth. Thanks, God. I know you're in this. We're all hurting, but I pray you continue to give me the strength and the right words to get us through this.

Jan dropped the girls off at school and went to the office. She spent the morning filing worship and Sunday school attendance records from the previous Sunday and helping Betty work through some financial issues. After a quick lunch she helped with the girls' Valentine's Day parties. When the school day ended, she took the girls, including Mary, to visit Wanda and her mom.

When they arrived, Carrie scampered out of the car with the box of valentines and ran toward the door with Sarah and Mary following. Jan followed more slowly and watched the girls run into the house. From outside, Jan could hear Wanda squeal with delight as Carrie gave her the valentines. Linda met Jan at the door. Wisps of hair escaped the sloppy ponytail that hung limply across Linda's back. Dark circles shadowed her eyes.

Hugging Linda, Jan said, "Not going to ask how you're doing, because I know you're hurting. But I'm here for you."

"Thanks, Pastor Jan," Linda said. "I just appreciate you and the church so much. I really don't know how I feel or what I'm doing."

Jan and Linda followed the girls into Wanda's bedroom. Wanda was sitting on the bed, surrounded by stuffed animals and books. Carrie, Sarah, and Mary combed through the box of valentines, giggling at the pictures and chattering about who had given Wanda which valentine. It was a picture not unlike the parties Jan had attended at the school earlier in the day, but different because the recipient of these valentines was pale, with thin strands of hair covering her head and sitting in a bed, not a school desk.

"I don't understand why this is happening," Linda whispered, wiping a tear from her eye."What did we do wrong? I know it's not right to question God, but why did this happen to us, to Wanda? She did nothing wrong."

Oh God, how do I respond to this?

Jan put her arm around Linda. "I don't understand, either. All I know is that God is with you and Tom, and also with Wanda. God will help us through this."

Jan's inadequate words wouldn't comfort Linda, which was frustrating. How could Jan comfort this family, this church, this town when she ached with her own grief? But she had to hold it together for everyone. Watching the girls giggling over the Valentine's Day cards, Jan flashed back to the dream that Carrie had had right before Christmas about Wanda. It was as if God were speaking to Jan right then through her child's dream. *Wanda was not alone anymore. She was safe and happy.* A tear slid down Jan's cheek and she quickly wiped it away. This would be hard. She had never done a child's funeral before, much less the best friend of her daughter. *Be with me, God.*

Bright flashes of light and booms of thunder startled Jan awake early the next morning. Wind whistled around the corner of the house and rain pounded the windows. Jan sat up, panicked, and listened to the live oaks in their yard bend and groan as branches thrashed against their home. She shivered. But it wasn't just the thunder and rain that had awakened her. A pulsating siren, starting loud, then growing soft, then loud again, blared over the storm. She glanced at the nightstand clock to see the time, 3:15, and the power blinked off. *What's going on?*

Ben groaned and sat up, rubbing his eyes. "Is that the town fire alarm?"

"Think so," she said, grabbing his hand as thunder exploded outside. "Power's out."

Ben got up and rummaged through the nightstand drawer for a flashlight. He turned it on and padded to the window.

"Looks like the whole town is out. But the lightning is so bad, we don't need the street lamps to see … I've never seen such a storm. Looks like one continuous flash." He paused and turned his head in the opposite direction. "I see an orange glow in the sky towards the school."

Jan's heart beat a little faster. *Fire.* She remembered the conversation she and Ben had with the fire chief about the pastor's role when the fire alarm went off. Though Baylorsville had a paid police and fire department, neither was large enough, so the town had volunteers, too. Soon after they'd moved to town, the town fire chief had visited them. He shared that, traditionally, the pastors of the town helped with both police and fire emergencies, but he didn't expect Jan to comply. Ben had glanced at his wife and said he would be happy to volunteer.

Jan and Ben had laughed about the conversation afterward, but Jan realized this was one more thing that worked against her as a woman pastor. She hadn't known whether to be upset or happy at subtly being told she wasn't expected to fight fires. But now fear crept into her consciousness. *What have I gotten Ben into? He's never fought a fire.* As the pastor of the Methodist Church, she should go, but she knew nothing about fighting fires, either. And what about the girls? She couldn't leave them in the middle of the night.

Ben glanced back at Jan, "You know I need to respond to the fire alarm."

Jan sat up in bed. "Ben, you don't need to do this. I'm sure they have enough people," she said, her voice cracking. She stepped to the window and put her arms around him. *God, Ben could get hurt.*

Two small squeals came from the girl's rooms and two sets of feet hit the floor as Carrie and Sarah fled down the hall and jumped into their parent's bed.

Jan went to the girls and pulled the covers over them. "It's okay, just a bad storm."

Ben picked up a pair of jeans and a shirt and started for the bathroom. "Jan, I need to be there. The other pastors will be there. And I'm not letting you go. I told the chief I'd respond."

"What's Daddy going to do, Mommy?" Carrie asked, peeking out from under the covers.

Before Jan could answer, the phone rang, causing her to jump. Ben turned toward her as she answered.

"Hi, Jim," she said. Jim was the chief of police and a member of First Church. "Yes, Ben's right here, he's already getting dressed." She looked into Ben's eyes. "Okay, I'll tell him, but do you really need him? Is it that bad?" At Jim's affirmative reply, Jan's heart raced. She hung up the phone and wrapped her arms around Sarah, who had started shivering.

"You were right, Ben," she said. Lightning flashed again and a loud clap of thunder startled them. The wind howled and rain pounded the window. "It's the elementary school. They think lightning hit it. The cafeteria is on fire and it's huge. They need lots of help. They want you to meet the police and fire trucks at the school."

Jan watched Ben button his shirt and pull on his socks and shoes. She got into bed and snuggled with her two little girls. "Are you sure you can do this? You've never fought a fire."

"Daddy, don't go," Sarah wailed. She jumped up from the bed and bear-hugged his legs.

"I'll be fine Sarah. I have to go help with your school." He untangled her arms from his legs and picked her up.

Carrie wrapped her arms around Ben, too, and looked into his eyes, "Will our school be okay, Daddy?"

Ben kissed her on top of her head. "Yes, Carrie, we'll make sure your school is okay."

Jan's heart beat hard. *But will Ben be okay?*

Seeing the girls so distraught, Jan realized she had to put her own fears and guilt aside to comfort them. "Hey, you two, let's sit in the kitchen and light candles." She would not be going back to sleep tonight. Likely no one would. She put on her robe and grabbed the flashlight from Ben. She and the girls followed Ben to the front of the house.

Before leaving, Ben knelt and hugged the two girls. "I'll be home later. You look after Mommy." He stood up and cupped Jan's chin. "I'll be fine, I promise. They probably won't let me anywhere near the fire. I'll just direct traffic or give out the coffee." He kissed her on the forehead. "Don't worry."

He grabbed another flashlight from a kitchen drawer, his rain jacket from a hook on the wall of the utility room, and headed out the side door. Jan stood by the door with the girls and watched him drive toward the fire. Lightning continued to flash, and she could see limbs strewn on the road in front of the house. Huge pine trees thrashed in the wind. A gust blew a branch into the carport and it skidded under her car. She shut the door as the sideways rain got them wet. *God, please keep Ben and the others safe.*

"Mommy, why's this happening? Will we be okay?" Carrie cried.

Jan looked at her shaking child. She was thinking the same thing. What was the morning going to bring to her family, to her small town? Would the school be burned to the ground? Would anyone be hurt? She knelt beside the girls and gathered them in her arms.

"When we are scared, what should we do?"

"Pray," they both said at once.

With Jan's arms still wrapped around them, she began. "Dear Jesus, we don't understand what's happening, but we know the police and the firefighters need help tonight. Protect them from the fire and storm. Be with Daddy as he helps. And be with the whole town. Help us get through this night. Amen."

"Amen," the girls echoed.

Jan had to distract the girls. She rummaged through the kitchen drawers and found two more flashlights. She silently thanked Ben, who, always the prepared Boy Scout, had put flashlights in strategic places throughout the house.

"Here, we'll take flashlights and make sure no rain is coming in the windows. Then we'll wait for Daddy in the den. I'll go get blankets and pillows and you can cuddle on the floor."

After the girls, snug in their blankets and pillows on the den floor, fell back asleep, Jan found their battery-operated radio and tuned it to the local Baylorsville station. The rather solemn announcer was assessing the damage. It seemed extreme, with reports of tree damage in town and the outlying county with major power outages. But the most serious damage so far seemed to be the fire at the Baylorsville Elementary School. There would be no school for these students today, nor in the near future.

She tried reading by candlelight at the kitchen table as she waited, but gave up. She ended up pacing, praying, and worrying about Ben.

Two hours later, car headlights turned into their driveway. Jan jumped up, her heart racing again, and jerked open the side door. Though the storm had eased, it was still raining. She peered through the gloom and recognized Ben's car. *Thank you, thank you, thank you.* She leaped out into the carport and hugged Ben as he got out of the car, nearly knocking him down.

"Thank God, you're here. Are you all right?" She took his soot-filled face in her hands.

"Of course, I'm okay. I told you I'd be fine. The pastors and I mainly gave everyone moral support."

Jan's heart sank. "Well, I could have done that." She turned, and went back into the dark kitchen, sinking into a chair. "I knew I should've gone."

"Oh, honey, it's okay," Ben said following her.

"No, it's not okay. What are the other pastors going to think about me now? And what about the church and the town? How will they respect me now?"

"Don't be silly, Jan. No one's going to think bad about you." He rested his head on his hands.

Jan paused for a moment, watching Ben. She realized he was tired and she was thinking only of herself. She took a deep breath and changed the subject.

"How's the school?"

Ben looked up. "It's bad. The school auditorium and cafeteria are just gone… burned right to the ground." He put his head on his arms. "At least no one was hurt, and we kept the fire from burning the rest of the school."

"Thank God." Jan remembered that the auditorium and cafeteria were later additions to the school and were not attached to the classrooms.

"How're the girls?" he asked, raising his head and looking into the den.

"They're fine. I gave them flashlights, and we checked the windows for leaks. They were afraid of the dark, but I told them all they had to do was go to the edge of the light. Once they got there, more light would show them the way."

"Wow, pretty profound," Ben said. "Guess there's no chance for a hot cup of coffee."

"Not 'til the power comes back on." She looked into the den at her sleeping children.

"Carrie and Sarah brought in their blankets and pillows, telling me they wouldn't go back to sleep." She smiled. "That lasted about five minutes. Did you go by the church?"

"Yeah, looks like branches in the parking lot and across the courtyard, but no major damage. I saw the power crews out. Hopefully the lights will be on soon. Is the phone still working?"

Jan picked up the phone. "Seems to be."

"Good, I need to check in with the college. Don't know if the storm hit Tallahassee, but even if it didn't, don't think I'll go in today." He looked at his watch. "Too early for anyone to be at the school. Think I'll take a shower first and then call." Ben smiled. "Hope the water is still hot."

Even though it was still raining, dawn was breaking. *O God, what will today bring? Thank you for being with Ben and the rest of the firefighters. Be with the school officials as they clean up this mess and be with the children. This will be a shock to them. Keep them safe.* She picked up a flashlight and followed Ben into the bedroom to get dressed. She needed to check on the church and her congregation and begin to make plans on how to respond to this new disaster. *God help us all.*

Chapter Eighteen

After the rain stopped later that morning, Jan and her family walked to the school. The smell of burned tar, wood, and fresh fallen pines created an acrid aroma that caused both Sarah and Carrie to hold their noses. When the school came into sight, Jan gasped. It was ruined. The entire roof had collapsed onto the floor of the cafeteria and it was just a shell of blackened walls. Both girls started crying. Kneeling and embracing her children, Jan shook her head. How would they ever get through this?

Yellow tape cordoned off the wreckage. The town fire truck was parked in front of the still-smoldering school. Several church members mingled in the crowd. Across the parking lot, children either sat on the ground or stood, clutching their parents' hands. All had shocked expressions, many were crying. Carrie broke away from Jan and ran over to them.

Jan's eyes swept across the crowd, and she noticed John Tully leaning against a pickup truck. He sipped from a Styrofoam cup. His clothes were rumpled and soiled. *What's he doing here?* Jan glanced at Ben and noticed him staring at John. She groaned under her breath when John walked toward them. She hoped he wouldn't taunt her about the fire.

"Thanks for your help last night, Professor," John said. He directed the statement to Ben, but he looked straight at Jan. "Appreciate you representing the Methodist church."

Jan felt her face turn red. She opened her mouth to respond, but Ben put his hand on her arm.

"No problem, glad to help." He guided Jan and Sarah away from John.

"Why didn't you let me answer him? He infuriates me," Jan fumed, sensing John's stare behind her back. "Now he'll spread it all over town that I didn't even have an excuse why I wasn't at the fire. I told you I should have gone. Everyone will think I couldn't handle this." Jan's hands shook as she grabbed Sarah's arm and turned away from the crowd, heading toward home.

"Mommy, what's wrong?" Sarah asked, looking up at Jan and almost stumbling as she tried to keep up with her mom.

"We're just going home, honey. Mommy's tired."

Ben caught up to them and put his hand on her arm. "Come on, Jan, calm down. No one will criticize you for staying home with the girls. No women were there last night."

"That's just it, Ben, no women were there!" Jan cried. She looked around her, mindful of the level of her voice, and said in a quieter tone. "But I should've been. All the pastors were there. The town will think I can't handle this job. Look how John reacted." Jan knew she was losing control. She walked away faster, almost dragging Sarah.

"Jan, please…" Ben caught up to Jan, but Carrie's voice stopped them. They both turned and saw Carrie running to them, with a young tow-headed boy following.

"Mom," Carrie said, "my teacher, Mrs. Hobbs, is over by the playground and she wants you to talk to the kids. They're all upset about the fire."

Jan and Ben glanced where Carrie was pointing. A dozen young children with a few adults surrounded the third-grade teacher. Many of the children were crying.

Jan stared at the children gathered around the teacher. *Get a hold of yourself. You came here to help. These children need you.* She knelt and hugged Carrie. "Sweetheart, tell your teacher I'll be right there."

She took a deep breath and stood. "Sorry, Ben, but John makes me so mad. I'm constantly having to prove myself to him."

"Well, doing your job includes comforting people and I think those people need comforting." He picked up Sarah, and they walked over to the growing crowd of parents and children around the picnic tables on the playground.

When Jan and Ben approached, Susie Green, a child in Carrie's third-grade class whose parents attended First Church, ran to them. Susie's eyes were red from crying and her voice shook. "Pastor Jan, Pastor Jan, look at our school. The fire burned it. Where are we going to go now? Why did this happen?" Susie threw her arms around Jan.

Jan knelt to receive Susie's hug. She took a seat at a picnic table and put Sarah on her lap as Carrie and Susie snuggled in beside her. "Well, Susie, I don't know why it happened, but I do know a bad storm caused lightning to start the fire." She sensed Ben nearby, silently giving her moral support. More people gathered around her, both children and adults. Jan's heart ached at the children's questions. They were frightened. Their safe place, the school, was blackened and ripped apart. Their world shattered in the storm. *Please give me the right words.*

"Does God still love us, Pastor Jan?"

Jan turned to Susie, cupping her chin and looking directly into her eyes. "Of course, God still loves us. God loves all of us. God was with us last night during the storm and God was with the police and the firefighters as they fought the fire." She looked up at the parents and children. "And God will continue to be with us. God will help your teachers and the principal make sure your school gets rebuilt." Susie's mother touched Jan's shoulder and whispered "thank you" in her ear. Jan was at the exact place she needed to be. She spent about half an hour with the children and their parents answering their questions and giving them moral support.

Later, when Jan and Ben got up to walk back home, Jan noticed John Tully standing by his truck, watching them. She couldn't read his expression, but it seemed he had been crying. *Wonder what he's still doing here.* She remembered what her friend, Sandy, said about talking to him. But she would handle him later, and they headed home.

Ben took her hand as Carrie and Sarah ran ahead. But as they started walking, Jan looked back at John. He was still standing by his truck, watching them. She stopped.

"Ben, I'll be right back." Before Ben could react, Jan headed back to John.

He was looking at the ground when she approached him.

"John, are you all right?"

He looked up, a puzzled expression in his eyes. "Uh, yes, Pastor Jan, just tired." He wiped his eyes. "Got to get home and get this fire dirt off me." He abruptly got in his truck and left.

Jan watched the truck leave and slowly walked back to Ben, who was staring at her.

"What was that about? I thought you were mad at him?"

"Well, he looked so sad." She continued to watch his truck leave. "Felt like I needed to ask if he was okay."

Ben took her hand again and laughed. "You continue to surprise me. Don't think I would have paid any attention to John. But, hey, what you did for those children was just as important as being at the fire."

Jan stopped, looked up at him, and smiled. "Thanks. I'm glad I could help calm them."

Her steps were light as they walked back home. "You know, Ben, you're right. I would've just stood around at the fire and watched."

"Yeah, kind of like me."

Jan punched him on the arm. "Come on, I know you did more than that. I'm sure they appreciated your help." She stopped again, observing their children skip down the sidewalk. "I know I helped the children and their parents this afternoon. But I also helped myself. Guess I needed an attitude adjustment from God reminding me of why I'm here."

"Well," he said, taking her hand and walking again, "it'll be a long week for everyone, so let's hope attitude adjustments are plentiful."

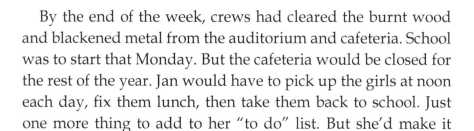

By the end of the week, crews had cleared the burnt wood and blackened metal from the auditorium and cafeteria. School was to start that Monday. But the cafeteria would be closed for the rest of the year. Jan would have to pick up the girls at noon each day, fix them lunch, then take them back to school. Just one more thing to add to her "to do" list. But she'd make it work.

Chapter *Nineteen*

That Thursday afternoon, three days after the fire, the girls quietly played in Jan's office while she worked on her sermon. School would be closed until Monday, and Carrie and Sarah had spent the morning at home with Ben. But they were bored, and Ben needed a break, so Jan took them to her office. She was in the midst of typing a paragraph when the outer office phone rang.

Betty's face said it all when she appeared at the study door. "It's Wanda."

Jan glanced at Carrie whose head had shot up with a questioning look. "Thanks, Betty. Girls, go into Miss Betty's office while I take this call, okay?"

"Mom, what's wrong?" Carrie asked. Jan went over and hugged her.

"I need to talk to Wanda's mom, Carrie. Go on into Miss Betty's office and I'll come get you in a minute." *Oh, God, this can't be good.*

Betty put her arms around both girls. "Come on. I think there're some chocolate chip cookies left over from Sunday. Let's go to the kitchen and find out."

Jan mouthed a silent "thank you" to Betty and, with her heart pounding, picked up the phone.

"Hello," Jan said, trying to sound confident and hopeful, but failing.

"Pastor Jan, she's gone." Linda's voice cracked as she spoke, but she was not hysterical. "Could you come to the house?"

Jan paled, and she gripped the phone harder. "Oh, Linda, I'm so sorry. I'll be there as quick as I can." She put the phone down and placed her head on the desk. Jan's mind whirled. *Oh, God, be with all of us.* She wondered why this happened so soon after the fire. Could she comfort the family and town when she hurt so, too? *Why, why, why?* She was crying.

She brushed her hair from her face, wiped the tears away, and made a mental list of what needed to be done. *First, I need to give Ben a quick call to come get the girls. Thank goodness he's home today. Then, I need … Oh God, what am I going to tell Carrie and Sarah? Carrie, especially, will sense something is wrong. How do I tell my child her best friend has just died?* She buried her face in her hands. Images of Wanda flashed through her mind: a spirited little girl with blond braids and freckles sprinkled across her face; the way Carrie pushed her high in the tire swing; the excited chatter of two eight-year-olds after the first day of school; Wanda's pale face after her surgery. Tears ran down Jan's cheeks as she grieved for this little girl and the loss of innocence that would come to this church, this town, and Carrie.

Oh, God, be with me. Let me be the conduit for your healing love and grace for all us as we go through the next few days. Be with Linda, Tom, and Mary. And especially be with my Carrie. She sat in her chair for a few more minutes, then picked up the phone and called Ben to get Carrie and Sarah.

While waiting for Ben, Jan headed toward the fellowship hall, where the kitchen was located. She stopped and watched Betty warming up the chocolate chip cookies in the microwave. Sarah had pulled a chair up to the counter and was watching the chocolate melt. She clapped her hands as the chime announced they were ready. Carrie was pulling milk out of the refrigerator. Jan didn't want to interrupt this normal scene. The world would tilt when she told her daughters Wanda had died.

She wished she could put a bubble around Sarah and Carrie and protect them from this grief. *O God, this is so not fair. Help me. Put the right words in my mouth.* Jan took a deep breath, walked across the fellowship hall, and entered the small kitchen.

Betty looked up and Jan gave her a quick nod. Betty put her hand over her mouth and gave a mumbled gasp. Jan went over to her daughters, took the plate of cookies from Betty, and set them on a table in the fellowship hall. Betty hugged her and hurried back into the office. Carrie carried two cups of milk and set them on the table, and looked up at Jan, her eyes asking the question her young mind was too afraid to ask. Sarah immediately crammed a cookie in her mouth. But Carrie just waited, studying her mom. Jan sat at the table and pulled Carrie into a hug.

She decided to be brutally honest. "Honey, Wanda just died."

Carrie said nothing, but her eyes twitched, and she jerked away from her mother. Sarah, sensing, but not understanding something was horribly wrong, silently came around the table and hugged Jan, smudging chocolate on her blouse. Jan ignored the chocolate stain and continued to watch Carrie, who had gone still. She desperately tried to find something to say to her child.

After about thirty seconds, which seemed like hours, Carrie shook herself and melted into Jan's arms.

"Mommy," she said, looking into Jan's teary eyes, "is Wanda in Jesus' arms now?"

Jan heard a sniffle from the direction of the office and saw Betty peeking around the office door, wiping her eyes. "Yes, honey, Wanda is now in Jesus' arms," Jan said, hugging both girls. "And Wanda is no longer sick."

"Then she can come out and play with us now, right Mom," Sarah piped up, grabbing the cup of milk and drinking. She left chocolate prints on the sides.

Jan sighed. How do you explain death to a five-year-old? "No, Sarah, she can't come out and play. She will stay with Jesus and God in heaven." Jan's heart was breaking, but she knew she had to make sure that both Carrie and Sarah understood that Wanda was dead. She didn't want either of them, or any of the other children, to think God had deliberately taken Wanda from them, though. She continued to hold her children close.

"Wanda was very sick. Her body just got too tired. So, God let Wanda come be with him."

"Forever?" Sarah asked.

"Yes, Sarah, forever." Sarah scrunched up her face. Jan sensed her little mind processing this information.

"Well, I don't like that." Sarah took another long drink from her glass of milk.

"I don't like it either," Carrie said. Tears were running down her face now and Jan held her tightly.

"I don't either, sweetie. I wish she had gotten better."

She saw Ben enter the fellowship hall behind the girls. He gave Jan a sad smile and turned to his daughters. His eyes, too, were red.

"Let's go home, girls." He grabbed the plate of cookies. "I bet Miss Betty won't mind if we take these home." He nodded to Betty as she came back into the fellowship hall.

"Nope, you go ahead and take them home. I'll clean up." Betty picked up the cups and napkins. She used one of the napkins to wipe her eyes.

Jan pecked Ben on the cheek. "Thanks. I'll be home … when I can." Her eyes followed them out the door.

Sweet God, I don't want to do this. Please be with my family. They need me now. But the Williams family needs me, too, and so does the church and community. Help me lead, O God.

She put Betty in charge of starting the prayer chain, which would alert the church and the town to this second tragedy, and grabbed her purse to head to the Williams' house.

Chapter Twenty

Jan breathed deeply, trying to calm herself, as she pulled her car in front of the Williams' small house. Guiding this family, church, and community through the funeral of a little girl would be the hardest pastoral challenge she had faced yet in Baylorsville. She wondered if she would be good enough. *Doesn't matter. It's my job. I have to do it.* She took another deep breath and got out of her car.

One of the town's police cars was parked haphazardly on the dirt driveway. In small towns, when people died at home, the police had to be present before the funeral home took the body. In this case, because it was an expected death, Wanda's doctor would have the attending police certify the death, which Jan supposed had already happened, because the funeral hearse was also in front of the house. As Jan climbed the steps to the Williams' house, she glanced toward the parsonage, only two houses away. Ben was just pulling into the carport, and she watched as he and the girls climbed out and headed into the house. Thankfully, neither of the girls saw her, but Ben did. He gave her a slight wave, and she lifted her hand. She felt a surge of relief as her two healthy daughters stepped into the house, quickly followed by a pang of guilt. She ran her hands through her hair. *Be with me, God, as I try to comfort this hurting family.*

Tom opened the door and motioned her in before she could

knock. She reached out to hug him, but he shook his head and walked away. *Be with him, God.*

Jan followed the sound of soft voices. She nodded to Pete Stellar, the youngest policeman on the Baylorsville six-person force, who was standing rock solid just outside Wanda's bedroom door. His eyes were red. He had probably never attended a death before. The funeral director, Bob Mullens, and his assistant, Jim Long, talked quietly in the hall beside the gurney. A small white folded sheet lay on top of it. Jan's heart broke and tears filled her eyes as she looked up at the two men, who'd stopped talking when she stepped into the hallway. Jan whispered a "thank you" and entered Wanda's room.

Linda was lying on the bed, propped up by pillows, rocking the now silent child in her arms. Jan wanted Wanda to look peaceful and sweet, only she looked pale, and gray. Death was not pretty, or kind, especially when it stole away a child. Anger flashed in Jan. *God, this is not right.* But she checked her emotions and embraced Linda.

After kissing Wanda's forehead, Jan prayed. "Oh God, we know Wanda is already in your arms. And we thank you she is now whole and healthy. But this family is hurting right now. Hold them close as they go through these next few days. Amen."

At a nod from the funeral director, Jan carefully coaxed Linda from the bed, so Wanda's body could be prepared to be taken to the funeral home. She guided Linda to the kitchen where they could sit and talk. Jan didn't want Linda to witness Wanda's body taken out of the house. She took Linda's hand in hers.

"Where did Tom go?" Jan asked Linda as they sat down. Jan had not seen him since he let her in the house.

Linda shook herself as if to wake up. Her eyes were red, and her voice trembled. "I … I don't know where Tom is." She looked around as if he were in the kitchen. "He was with me when Wanda, uh, stopped breathing… Oh, God, I can't handle this, my baby, my baby." She broke down again.

Jan held her but didn't speak. *This is so painful, God. Help us get through this.*

After a few moments, Jan rose and grabbed some tissue from the kitchen counter and handed them to Linda. "I'll go find Tom. Is Mary here?"

Linda wiped at her eyes and blew her nose. "No, Mary is with my sister, Lucy. She drove over from Dothan this morning. I think she took Mary to the park. Oh, Pastor Jan, how am I going to tell Mary? What am I going to tell Mary?" Linda's sobs all but drowned out the sound of the doorbell.

Jan realized people were finding out about this death. In this small town, neighbors would already be coming with food, tears, and hugs. Many would need comfort, too. Jan gave Linda a hug again and went to answer the door.

The town doctor was at the door. *Good, maybe he can give Linda something to calm her.*

"Hi, Dr. Walker." Jan shook his hand.

"Sad thing here, Pastor Jan, but glad it's over," he said. They both observed the funeral hearse backing into the street. "Are Linda and Tom inside?"

"Linda is, in the kitchen. I'm looking for Tom."

"I'll go check on Linda," Dr. Walker said, heading toward the kitchen.

"Thanks for coming, Dr. Walker. They will certainly appreciate the visit."

Another car pulled into the driveway. Two women from the church got out with casseroles in their hands. A fleeting thought of casseroles being thawed right now from dozens of freezers had Jan almost laughing before she caught herself. *God, how can I even think that at a time like this?* But it was a bit comical to think of people keeping dishes to quickly respond to a crisis. *No it's not comical, it's what makes small towns special.* She let the women in, hugged them, and directed them to put the dishes on the dining room table.

This is going to be a zoo. She had to find Tom, and especially Mary. She didn't want Mary to hear of her sister's death from anyone but her mom and dad. Jan walked around the corner of the house and saw Tom leaning up against a tree in the back yard. He was alone, and Jan approached him.

"Tom, I'm so sorry," she said.

Tom looked up and rubbed his swollen eyes. "I really expected she'd get better."

Suddenly, he slammed his fist into the tree. "Damn it."

Jan flinched as Tom looked at his bloody knuckles.

Shaking his hand, he said a bit calmer, "How can a loving God take a baby? I don't understand, I just damn don't understand." He sighed and shook his head. "I'm sorry, Pastor Jan, but I hate Him right now. If God is so almighty and powerful, why didn't God save her? Why'd He take my baby girl?" he yelled with tears streaming down his cheeks.

Jan took his hand, examined it to check for an injury, and led him to a chair propped up against the house. "I don't understand either, Tom. And it's okay to be angry at God. God can certainly take it." She knelt beside him. "I don't know why God didn't answer our prayers the way we wanted. But I do know God is crying with us right now. God understands we hurt, and God's in this." Jan looked into Tom's eyes.

"Pastor Jan. I just may be through with God for now."

"God understands that, too."

Tom stood and swiped at his angry eyes. "I need to check on Linda. And I've got to call my parents and find Mary. Lucy took her to the park." He walked to the rear kitchen door but turned and said, "Thank you, Pastor Jan. You've really been here for us. I don't want to upset you, but I just need … " He couldn't finish.

"It's alright, Tom. I'll be here for you whatever you need. Go to Linda. I'll find Lucy and bring Mary to you." She stared at him as he shuffled toward the door. *God, I hope I helped some. He's so angry and I don't blame him. I'm angry too. Be with us in all of this.* She left to find Mary. This was going to be a long afternoon.

Jan found Mary holding hands with Lucy, a younger, shorter version of Linda, walking from the lake.

On seeing Jan, Mary immediately dropped Lucy's hand and sprinted toward Jan."Pastor Jan, Pastor Jan, look what I found at the lake." Mary clutched a large feather in her hand and waved it close to Jan's face. Jan smiled at the bubbly child and picked her up, examining the feather. Amidst Mary's excited chatter, Jan glanced at Lucy, and mouthed, "Wanda's gone."

Lucy put both hands over her mouth and gasped, "Oh no, how're we going to get through this?"

Jan put Mary down and hugged Lucy. "We'll all help you." She glanced down at Mary who was staring up at her aunt. "Tom's looking for Mary."

Each grabbed one of the little girl's hands and they walked back to the Williams' house.

Several cars were already lining the front lawn as they approached the house. Mary pulled on their hands, causing them to stop.

"Why are all these cars here?" she asked.

Jan looked at Lucy. "Let's go in the kitchen door. Linda's there."

Going around to the back yard, they opened the kitchen door, finding Tom talking on the phone with his arm around Linda. Lucy rushed to Linda, and both collapsed, crying. Mary looked up at her mom and her aunt and burst into tears, too.

"Mama, what's wrong? Why is everyone here? Why're you crying?"

Jan's heart broke again. It was all she could do to keep from crying herself. Linda gave her sister a tight squeeze and turned to Mary as Tom put the phone down. Both Tom and Linda bent down to their distraught daughter. Linda looked at up Jan, her eyes asking, "how do we tell her?"

Jan motioned for them to sit at the table. She looked at Linda and Tom and said, "Tell her the truth. She already knows."

Tom sat at the table and took Mary into his lap. Linda knelt beside them and took her tiny hands into her own.

"Baby," Linda said, her voice cracking, "Wanda has gone to be with God."

Jan watched Mary's eyes as they darted back and forth between her mother and father. Her forehead scrunched up and her lips quivered. Jan knew Mary was reacting more to her parent's anguish than the stark reality of her sister's death. She flashed back to Sarah's reaction, thinking because Wanda was no longer sick and with Jesus that she could now come out and play again. How does a five-year-old understand a beloved sister would never play again? Tom and Linda wrapped their arms around Mary as she whimpered, and it was too much for Lucy as she erupted in loud sobs. Jan silently watched, her heart aching.

Once Mary had calmed down, Lucy took her outside and Jan carefully began the process of preparing this young couple for their daughter's funeral. Because it was a Thursday, and the cemetery was not open on weekends, the family decided to have the service on Monday morning. It would be a long weekend for everyone. After several minutes of planning, Linda and Tom left the kitchen to continue grieving with their friends who had been gathering in the small living room. Following them, Jan noticed the feather Mary had found lying on the floor. Jan picked it up and held it to her face, then placed it on the kitchen table. Perhaps it would give Mary some comfort.

Ben was preparing supper when Jan returned home late that afternoon. She walked into the house to the rich smell of frying chicken.

"Thought I'd take care of this for you," he said.

"Thanks," she said pecking him on the cheek. "Love your fried chicken, but I'm really not very hungry."

"I know." Ben pulled her into a hug. "But you've got to eat, and the girls are hungry. We all need some comfort food right now. How are Tom and Linda?"

"'Bout as you'd expect. We all knew this was coming, but it just seems so surreal. Tom's really taking it hard. He's angry."

"That's probably good," Ben said, turning the chicken in the frying pan. "He's really been silent about his feelings." He glanced at Sarah, who was watching TV in the den. "I can't imagine losing one of our girls. Wanda was his baby. He's got to be mad."

"Yeah, it's hard to see him so upset. But, I don't blame him. I'm mad, too." She looked at Sarah in the den. "Where's Carrie?"

"She's outside on the swing watching the people go into the Williams' house. She's talking about it some, but she's hurting."

Jan stepped to the kitchen window and studied Carrie, who was swinging on the tree swing. She ached for her child. *Oh, God, what can I say to Carrie. I just wish it never happened.* A single tear fell from Jan's eye. *I can't say anything, God, except we're hurting. Perhaps that's all I need to say.* A plan for what she would say during the funeral service began to form in Jan's mind. These people were looking for her leadership, and with God's help, she would be that leader. Taking a deep breath, Jan slipped into the backyard to comfort her daughter.

Chapter Twenty-One

Friday was a chaotic day. Jan spent the morning putting the final touches on her Sunday sermon and preparing the memorial service. But she also had to juggle her time with the girls as Ben was in Tallahassee for his classes. So, Carrie and Sarah, somewhat reluctantly, spent the morning in her office again. The girls were definitely affected by Wanda's death. Reading and coloring, usually their favorite activities, didn't calm them, and they were aloof, whiny, and moody. Fortunately, a mom of a school friend invited them to play in the afternoon, which improved their moods and allowed Jan to spend much of the afternoon at the Williams' home comforting family members who had come into town.

By the time Saturday arrived, Jan was exhausted. But she knew it would not be the day of rest she needed. The service on Sunday would be difficult enough with the aftermath of the fire, and now she had to embrace a congregation grieving over the loss of a child. Even though everyone had expected Wanda's death, it was still a shock. How did anyone prepare for the death of a child?

Jan needed peace and quiet and thought a walk around the lake would provide her the strength she needed for the next few days. Her sermon for the next day was nearly ready, but the meditation for Wanda's funeral was just starting to form in her mind. It would take several hours of thought to put that on paper. She stepped onto the path and, with her head bowed, started her walk.

"Pastor Jan, Pastor Jan."

Jan's heart sank as she turned and Randi Fox, with her two young sons, came running toward her. *So much for my solitude.*

Jan stopped and waited for them.

"Oh, Pastor Jan, this is terrible. Poor Linda and Tom. And that poor sweet child." Randi threw her arms around Jan, almost knocking her down, and burst into tears.

Though she needed this time for herself, Jan couldn't help but respond to the hug and Randi's tears. Even the two little boys burst into tears. Jan hugged Randi and knelt to embrace the little boys. "I know, Randi, this is so hard. Just keep the Williams family in your prayers." She watched Randi, still crying, lead her children to the playground. *Everyone is in so much pain.*

Jan continued her walk and had almost made it around the lake when two other church members came hurrying toward her. *Think I will have to find another quiet place.* Jan stopped as they approached her. Miles and Susie Hillsbrook both taught at the elementary school. Naturally, they were upset about the fire and Wanda's death. She spent a while listening to their pain, hugging them, and praying with them. She stared at them as they walked off and a tear ran down her cheek. At first, she resented having to spend her quiet time comforting these people, but running into Randi and the Hillsbrooks were, in fact, God interruptions. Jan finished her walk and headed to the church with a renewed sense of peace and direction. God, through these sweet people, had given her the perfect message, not only for Sunday, but for the funeral of little Wanda.

Instead of going to her study, she spent time in the church sanctuary. She entered the side door and breathed in the familiar smells of burnt candles, flowers, perfume, and the mustiness of an old building. *I love this place.* She sat in the front pew, letting the ambiance of the sanctuary fill her before she got up and headed to her study to continue the preparations.

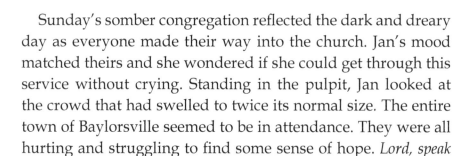

Sunday's somber congregation reflected the dark and dreary day as everyone made their way into the church. Jan's mood matched theirs and she wondered if she could get through this service without crying. Standing in the pulpit, Jan looked at the crowd that had swelled to twice its normal size. The entire town of Baylorsville seemed to be in attendance. They were all hurting and struggling to find some sense of hope. *Lord, speak through me to these broken people.*

She started the service with the words from Romans 8:31 and hoped this verse from the Bible would bring comfort. "'What should we say to all of this? If God is for us, who can be against us?... Who shall separate us from the love of Christ? Shall tribulation, or distress, or persecution, or famine, or nakedness, or danger, or sword? No, in all these things we are more than conquerors through him who loved us.'"

Her eyes moved across the swelled congregation, and she almost gasped as she noticed John and Martha Tully, partially hidden in the far left corner of the room. They had not been to church since that fateful conversation in her office in the fall. *Oh, no, I hope he's not here to make trouble.* Flustered, with her heart beating a little quicker, she continued reading the scripture.

"'For I am sure that neither death nor life, nor angels nor rulers, nor things present nor things to come, nor powers, nor height nor depth, nor anything else in all creation, will be able to separate us from the love of God in Christ Jesus our Lord.'"

Closing the Bible, she breathed deeply, hoping the Tullys presence would not distract her. She lifted up a silent *be with me* and started preaching.

"We, in our small town, have experienced a great loss this past week. The storm, and the damage it did, especially to the elementary school, and now the death of sweet Wanda, have us asking God, why? Why did these terrible things happen?

Where is the hope in all this? Where is God?"

She paused a moment, more to center herself than to make a point. "Well, folks, I don't think the hope of our world can be found in the earthly, worldly stuff we find around us. In fact, I don't think the world as it exists today can offer much hope that things will be okay. Storms happen, and not just the storms of nature. Life can be cruel. Accidents happen, jobs are lost, relationships break up … and children die."

Her voice cracked, and she paused amidst the soft cries coming from the congregation. She again looked out at the crowd, focusing on these people she now called friends. She sighed and continued.

"But I do know God is with us in these tragedies. In fact, God is crying right now with us because God knows what it's like to lose someone. God lost his son, Jesus." Jan felt a deep connection to the congregation now. They were listening.

"During the storm when the lights went out, Carrie and Sarah were scared, as I'm sure all of your children were. After Ben left to help with the fire, I gave the girls flashlights and we checked for leaks at the windows. They were afraid of the dark, so I told them all they had to do was go to the edge of the light, and when they got there, they would see more light. They would never have to be without the light. It would always guide them. My analogy worked, and we got through that horrible night."Jan looked at Carrie and Sarah, and they both smiled.

"But afterwards," Jan continued, "I thought about that light." She gazed across her congregation. "My friends, we have all been in a very dark place in our lives. With the fire and now the death of little Wanda, the edge of darkness seems vast and scary and even forever. But Jesus, as the light, knows all about our fear of the edge of that darkness. He does not ask us to penetrate the darkness. All he asks is that we go to the edge, and he will meet us with more light. This has been a horrible week for us. The darkness is still with us. We can't deny that these tragedies have happened. We hurt and we will hurt for a long time.

But God, through Jesus, will continue to provide the light at the edge of that darkness for us. That light is our hope, my friends. That light is how we go on from here."

As Jan ended her sermon, she gazed at her congregation. Many were crying.

Stepping away from the pulpit, she nodded to the choir director to lead the congregation in the last song. She felt good about the sermon. Hopefully the message would give these people comfort. Then her attention was caught by a movement in the rear of the church. The Tullys were leaving. Her anxiety kicked in. Did they not like what she said? Had she not been able to help them? But she brushed the thought off. She was doing the best she could do. She didn't have time to worry about them now. She made a mental note to call them later in the week.

The congregation stood, and Jan joined them in the singing of the song, "Hope of the World."

Ben and Jan walked with their girls back to the house. Carrie ran ahead as usual with Sarah doing her best to keep up.

"Good job, Jan," Ben said. "That must have been hard."

"Yeah, it was." She slipped her hand in his. "But it was healing for me, too. As I saw everyone responding to the worship service, it helped me, gave me hope that together we can get through this."

"Well, you sounded very confident. Lots of folks were touched by your light story."

"That was a God thing," Jan said, picking up on one of their favorite expressions. When something clicked or just worked for either of them, they claimed that God had done it.

Jan and Ben spent the rest of the day quietly. The girls played in their rooms, Ben watched a college basketball game on TV, and Jan napped. It was a normal, restful Sunday afternoon, and they all needed that breather. The next day would be hard with Wanda's funeral.

Chapter Twenty-Two

Wanda's funeral was set for ten Monday morning. Ben stayed home from work to attend the service with Carrie and Sarah. Though Jan and Ben didn't want their daughters attending a funeral at so young an age, they both felt it was necessary in this case. Jan knew the service would be full of children, as the school principal had delayed reopening the school until Tuesday.

Jan walked to the church before eight that morning, eyeing the lake as she passed, wishing she had time to walk. But she continued toward the church and entered the sanctuary, going directly to the altar rail and kneeling. The funeral home would bring the small casket about nine, and Jan wanted to spend some quiet moments in prayer before then.

God, be with us all, but especially me. I don't want to break down in front of the town and this congregation, but this is so hard for me. Help us all get through this.

She looked up as the door to the sanctuary opened and Betty walked in with flowers.

"Oh, sorry, Pastor Jan. I didn't know you were here," she said. "These just arrived, and I wanted to place them just right." She started for the altar but burst into tears before she got there.

"This is just so unfair," Betty sobbed.

Jan jumped up from the altar rail and met her coming down

the aisle. "I know," Jan said, hugging Betty. "But God will get us through this."

⟶ ⟫⟩▸◆◂⟨⟪ ⟵

An hour later, Jan stood at the top of the sanctuary steps. Tears sprang to her eyes as the funeral directors pulled the small pink casket out of the hearse and into the waiting arms of the four pallbearers, large burly men who worked with Tom. *Oh, my God, that's a child in there, a little girl I loved, my daughter's best friend.* Jan turned her face away from the pallbearers. *I can't break down.* She took three deep breaths and blinked back the tears. But watching the four men shift into position and walk the casket up the steps of the church wrenched her heart. *That could be Carrie or Sarah.*

She stepped in front of the casket when the men reached the top step leading into the sanctuary, and mentally shaking herself, she began the long walk down the church aisle. The pallbearers followed, carrying the casket, with Wanda's family coming last. Small town funerals were quite ritualistic, and this funeral was no different. It was like a choreographed play. Everyone had a place and a part. Jan hoped that the familiar rote of the funeral rituals would numb her enough to get through the service without breaking down. She needed to be strong. People were depending on her.

Jan stopped at the front of the chancel and waited for the family, watching as they hesitantly moved down the aisle. Linda, whose eyes were red, held tightly to Mary's hand. Tom walked slightly behind Linda and Mary, as if protecting them from this tragedy. He stoically stared straight ahead, his mouth a tight, hard line. After the casket was placed in front of the altar, Jan went over to Linda and Tom, ushering them and the rest of their family into the left front pew. Before she turned to go to the pulpit, she leaned down and kissed Mary on the head.

As expected, there were many children in the congregation. Ben, Carrie, and Sarah were sitting in their usual right front pew. She met Ben's eyes, and he gave her an encouraging nod. But Carrie was crying, and tears sprang again to Jan's eyes. She wished she could wrap her arms around her child. *Be with Carrie, my God. Hold her in the palms of your hands as we go through this service.* Jan swiped quickly at her tears, took a deep breath, and seated the congregation.

She went through the funeral prayers, said the scriptures, and did the eulogy, all the while listening to the cries from the congregation. At the end of the service, she stepped from the pulpit and knelt before the Williams family. "Wanda loved you very much. And we know you loved her, too. But before she was yours, she was God's." Jan stood and looked at the congregation. She prayed. "Oh, God, for all that Wanda has given us to make us what we are, for that of Wanda which lives and grows in each of us to make us what we are, and for her life that in your love will never end, we give you thanks. As we offer her back into your arms, comfort us in our loneliness and grief, strengthen us in our weakness, and give us the courage to face the future unafraid. In Jesus' name. Amen."

Guided by the funeral directors, the pallbearers stepped in front of the small casket and carried it back down the church aisle. Jan followed, ushering the family through the church. She glanced at Ben, who was hugging Carrie. Sarah looked up as Jan passed and smiled. But the smile had no joy in it. Jan swallowed back her tears.

About thirty cars, long for a funeral procession in this small town, followed the funeral coach as it carried the body of Wanda to her final resting place. The cemetery was on the outskirts of town.

Jan's voice broke as she uttered the final prayers. At the end of the committal service, everyone was given a rose to put on the casket. Tom and Linda went first, but little Mary, confused and tired, balked when Linda prompted her to leave the flower on top of her sister's casket. The small child burst into tears and jerked away from her mother, with the pink rose in her hand.

"No, I want to save it for Wanda," she screamed, running through the tombstones, away from the crowd.

Linda sank to the ground, putting her hands over her eyes. Tom glanced toward Mary, and seeing that Lucy, her aunt, had followed his child, put his arm around Linda and helped her up. By this time, many of the forty or so people who had attended the committal service were crying as they continued to place roses on the small casket.

The crowd gradually dispersed after giving their condolences to Linda and Tom. Jan stood beside the family, trying to offer comfort to them as well as the crowd. After most of the people had left, the funeral directors ushered Tom and Linda back to the funeral car. Lucy was standing there, holding Mary. Jan went up and hugged the little girl. The pink rose was still clutched in her hand.

Jan watched as the funeral car pulled away. She was grateful the family had decided not to have a reception, which was normal in this part of the country after a funeral. She glanced back at the funeral tent and saw the grave diggers lowering the casket into the grave. She sighed and climbed into her own car. She was exhausted and wanted to go home and hug her family.

Tuesday, the elementary school reopened, and the girls went back to school. Jan began her day by walking around the lake, trying to process all that had happened at the funeral. As she walked, she reflected on the conversation she'd had with Tom the Saturday before the funeral. Tom was still very angry and had proclaimed that he would not forgive God for taking his child. Jan responded by telling him about a friend, whose husband had suddenly died. The friend realized that on her own, she could not forgive God for letting her husband die, only God could help her forgive. This insight had helped her friend heal. After Jan had finished telling Tom this story, he had only nodded his head and walked away. Jan wondered how much she had helped him. She suddenly stopped walking as those words "only God could help her forgive" echoed again in her mind. Jan could talk with Tom, could pray for him, could literally hold his hand, but ultimately, she would have to trust that only God could help him. Jan smiled as she started walking again. Yes, God would help Tom through this terrible grief, but perhaps God was using Jan to help, too.

In her office on Tuesday morning, Jan sat down with a cup of coffee. She was getting ready to start typing her sermon when the phone rang. She flinched, hoping it was not another crisis. She needed some respite from the chaos of the fire and the anguish of Wanda's death. But that was not going to happen. She heard Betty answer the phone.

"Sure, Martha, Pastor Jan is in. Hold on and I'll get her."

Betty knocked, opened the door, and shook her head. "Martha Tully wants to speak with you. I hope this isn't more bad news."

Jan grimaced and mouthed "me too" as she picked up her phone. "Hi, Martha."

Martha didn't mince any words. She started right in with her request. "Pastor Jan, John and I would like to meet with you. Can you come out to our house this afternoon?"

Jan's heart raced. Seeing Martha and John at both the Sunday service and the funeral that week flashed through her mind. What did they want and why did they want her to come to their house? "Sure, Martha. What time?"

"How about 2:00?"

"Ok, that'll be great. It will give me a chance to get the girls back to school after lunch. See you then." Jan put the phone down and noticed that Betty had left the door to the outer office open. She stared at Jan with her hand over her mouth.

"They want you to come to their house?" Betty asked.

"Yep."

"They were at the funeral, weren't they?"

"Yeah, they were. They were also in church on Sunday." Jan rested her head on her hands. "I don't know whether to be excited or scared."

Betty shook her head. "Good luck. I'll pray for you."

"Thanks," Jan said. Betty shut the door and Jan sank into her chair. She hoped they wouldn't find fault with the funeral. She didn't think she could deal with any more drama. But her curiosity was piqued, too. She thought back to the way John looked at her the day of the fire after she had talked to the children. Maybe she would finally find out what was going on.

Chapter Twenty-Three

After lunch, Jan dropped the girls at school and drove to the Tullys' house. Still emotionally and physically tired from the funeral, she didn't want to battle John right now. But she was also curious about this unusual summons. *Lord, be with me.*

Overnight the weather had turned warmer, and she rolled down her windows. It was one of those lazy, early spring days, quite different from the dreary weekend. She pulled into the Tullys' long, red-dirt drive and breathed deeply, hoping to calm her rapidly beating heart. The rich smell of pine, the faint acrid smell of the marshy meadows, and the sweet earthy aroma of newly mowed grass picked up her rather edgy spirits. But the tension returned when she pulled up to the house and John and Martha came out onto the front porch. Jan wiped her sweaty hands on her skirt and got out of the car.

Dear God, please give me strength for whatever will happen right now. Help me keep my cool.

"Hi, John, Martha. Isn't it a lovely day?" She shut the car door and made her way up the steps.

"Yes, it's beautiful out, especially after that horrible storm," Martha said. She smiled and appeared calmer and less timid than Jan had ever seen her. John hovered behind her. He acted differently, almost timid. He was wearing an old pair of jeans, a faded flannel shirt with the sleeves rolled up, and scuffed, dirty tennis shoes. She had never seen him in anything but dress clothes.

"Come in, Pastor Jan," John said as he opened the door and ushered her inside. "Let's sit outside on the deck." John led her through a house that was much nicer than most of her parishioners' houses. Soft colors of blues and browns dominated the classical furnishings. Redwood paneling covered one wall. A blue oriental rug adorned the vast great room and a stone fireplace with a long, handmade mantle covered the back wall.

Jan tingled with nervousness, even as she admired the home. They obviously had money.

"Pastor Jan, would you like some sweet iced tea?"

"Sure, Martha, thanks," Jan said as John led her to the back of the house. A cool breeze drifted in from the open French doors. They stepped out onto a tiered wooden deck, which overlooked Lake Seminole. A well-tended lawn with huge pine trees flowed down to the lake's shore. Several trees had fallen.

John followed her gaze. "The storm took down about ten of my pine trees. I've been busy cutting them up. It's hard work." He looked down at his work clothes and shrugged.

"I bet it is. Sorry you lost the trees. Looks like you've done a great job of cutting them up."

Martha came out of the kitchen carrying an ornate tray with three glasses of iced tea and a plate of sugar cookies. "Let's sit over here, Pastor Jan," she said, putting the tray on a glass table tucked between two wooden rocking chairs facing the lake. Jan sat in one as John sat on a free-standing wooden swing angled toward the lake. Martha sat in the other rocking chair.

"John and Martha, your house is lovely, and this view is amazing. It's so peaceful here." Jan sipped her tea, listening to the birds singing and hearing the gentle lapping of the lake water. Normally, water relaxed her. Not today. She wondered what they wanted.

"Yes, we love it here," Martha said.

"How long have you lived here?" Jan asked, making pastoral small talk as she put the glass on the table and picked up a cookie.

"We built the house just over ten years ago, after…" Martha said, but John raised his hand to shush her.

"Pastor Jan, that's what we want to talk to you about."

Jan's heart quickened. She worried John would get into another screaming rage. Her mind flashed to the day after the fire when John stared at her as she and her family left. But John didn't get angry. He leaned over to Martha and touched her hand. Martha smiled and tightened her fingers around his. Jan lifted a cookie to her mouth.

"First, I want to apologize," John said. He dropped Martha's hand and took a deep breath.

Even though Jan had taken a small bite of the cookie, she still almost choked. She took a sip of tea. She sure had not expected an apology.

"I've treated you horribly, and I'm so sorry," John continued.

Jan started to speak, but John cut her off. His face had turned ashen.

"Please, let me finish. This is hard for me. I haven't told anyone about this and I just need to get it out."

"Oh, of course, John. Go on." Jan looked at Martha and saw tears forming in her eyes. *What's going on here?* Jan sat back in her chair and waited for John to continue.

He put his elbow on the side of the swing, and his fingers touched his forehead. He sighed. "It's been twelve years since we lost our daughter, Sarah." His voice broke. "She was only nine when she died of complications relating to cancer."

Jan gasped and put her hand over her heart. "I'm… I'm so sorry, John, Martha," she said glancing at Martha, who was staring at John.

John put his hand up again, cutting Jan off from saying anything else. "It was a bad time for us. We tried everything: took her to the best doctors, got her the best medicine, but in the end, she just couldn't get her strength back."

He stood and walked to the end of the deck, facing the water. Jan's eyes followed him. *Oh, my goodness.* Realization shook her. It was grief over their daughter's death that had caused John's mean attitude.

Still staring at the lake, John continued, "When I heard you were coming to our town, I must admit I was anxious about a woman pastor, but when I found out one of your daughters' name was Sarah, something inside of me died all over again." His voice broke again as he sobbed.

Martha seemed to grow larger and straighter as she got up and put her arm around him. They were both crying now. Jan stayed in her chair, watching them. She wished they had told her about their daughter months ago. They were grieving all over again with Wanda's death. *Oh, my God, how do I help them?*

John and Martha held each other. Jan remained quiet, instinctively knowing to give John space. The sun warmed her as she once again listened to the birds singing, the wind softly sweeping through the trees, ducks quacking on the water. After several minutes, John cleared his throat and wiped his eyes. He squeezed Martha's hand and walked back toward Jan.

"Pastor Jan, again, I need to apologize. I've treated you so badly."

Jan attempted to speak and as before, John put up his hand to stop her talking and sat in the swing.

"Please, let me continue, Pastor Jan." He looked up as Martha came to join him. He put his arm around her. "I guess I thought I could protect myself," he looked at Martha, who smiled at him, "we could protect ourselves, by moving here and forgetting about Sarah's death. Nobody here knew us. We wouldn't have to talk about it." He grew quiet for a moment. "I threw myself into building this house." He glanced at the lake. "And I bought a boat and learned to fish. It worked for a few years. But then you came, with a daughter named Sarah. And then Wanda died, and it all came back." He started crying again.

Jan got up this time, knelt beside them, and took their hands.

"I'm so sorry for you both. I can't imagine what you must have gone through."

John cleared his throat again, let go of Jan's hand and stood up, nearly knocking her over. "Well, enough of this." He rubbed his eyes with his hand. "Again, I'm sorry for the way I've been acting. I hope you'll forgive me. Martha and I'll be coming back to church, and I'd like to take the treasurer's job again if you'll have me." He moved toward the rail and again looked toward the lake.

Jan almost laughed. Once John got the apology out of the way, he reverted back to his old abrupt ways. But she got hold of her emotions and said, "Of course I'll forgive you, John. I hope you'll forgive me, too. I should've been more aware of your pain." Although she was not a mind reader and could not possibly have known about their daughter. "But as for the treasurer, I must run it through the church council first." *And things will change. You will not bully me anymore.*

Jan sat back down in the rocking chair and picked up her glass of tea. She waited while John struggled to control his emotions.

But it was Martha who spoke. "Our Sarah was such a sweet little thing. We were older when she was born, in our late thirties. We never thought we would have children." Martha looked at John, who continued to stare out at the lake. She glanced back at Jan. "And we were elated when she came into our lives. Sarah was the light of our world. She loved to sing and would break out in song at a moment's notice. When she got sick, it just devastated us." Martha's voice cracked and her face crumbled, the tears falling again.

Jan's heart broke. *Oh God, I want to help her.* She wanted to fix them but knew all she could do was listen.

John left the deck rail and sat again beside Martha, putting his arm around her. "We don't know Linda and Tom well. But when Wanda died, we..." Again, he looked at Martha and took her hand as Martha smiled at him. "... I knew we had to get over our own pain and make things right with you, the church, and especially the Williams family." John looked right into Jan's eyes now. "What can we do to help them?"

Jan blinked, stunned. But she mentally shook herself and said, "Talking to them and sharing your story would really help. What a gift you can give them, to remind them they're not alone in their pain. Would you be willing to tell them about losing Sarah?"

John and Martha looked at each other. John nodded and Martha smiled, saying, "Yes, Pastor Jan, we'd be happy to talk with them."

"Well, Pastor Jan," John said, standing. "You arrange the when and where."

Jan could tell this conversation was over. The controlling John was back. But there was a softer edge to him now.

"Sure, John. I need to be going. The girls will be home from school soon." She hesitated. "Can I pray with you?"

"Yes, please pray with us," Martha said.

They stood and held hands as Jan prayed on that beautiful deck, amidst the warmth of the sun, the singing of the birds and the sweet smell of pine.

Jan's thoughts swirled as she left the Tullys' home and took the long, curvy drive back to town. *Oh God, how you have spoken to me today. Thank you for reminding me that often when people seem to be rough and angry, they have had horrible things that have happened to them. How awful for the Tullys, but how wonderful that you opened their hearts to help the Williamses. Forgive me for being so hard on John and forgive him for being so hard on me. Help this be healing for everyone. Amen.*

Chapter Twenty-Four

That evening, Jan shared the Tullys' sad story with Ben.

"I need to keep this confidential, but I had to tell you." Jan stirred the pasta sauce as Ben tossed the salad. "I just wish they had told me this months ago. I feel a little guilty for being so mad at John. He was really hurting."

"Well, I wouldn't worry about those guilty feelings," Ben said, putting his arm around Jan. "He was pretty mean to you."

"Yeah, you're right. But I'm glad God is using Wanda's death, as horrible as it is, to help John and Martha face their own grief."

"So, how will you handle this?" Ben put silverware on the table, and Jan put the noodles and sauce on plates and set them on the placemats.

"I'll make sure Tom and Linda get together with the Tullys. I'm sure Linda would love to talk with Martha. Not so sure about Tom. I'm really concerned he'll clam up and keep everything locked inside him. But if I can get Tom and John together, maybe something good can happen for them both." *At least I hope so.*

"Sounds like it might work," Ben said. He stepped into the den and called the girls to dinner.

"Wow, spaghetti," Carrie exclaimed as she scurried into the dining room, Sarah on her heels. "I love spaghetti."

"Me, too," Sarah piped in, always mimicking her sister.

They prayed together and both girls dove into their food. Jan looked at Carrie, glad she was eating. It had been a tough week for her.

"Hey mom," Carrie said, wiping spaghetti off her mouth, "we've been studying butterflies at school. My teacher said if you plant certain kinds of flowers, they'd attract butterflies." She picked up her glass of milk. "Can we plant a butterfly garden?"

"Sure," Jan said. A thought popped into her head as she sipped her tea. "Hey," she said setting her glass down. "I have a great idea. How about we plant a butterfly garden at the church in memory of Wanda?"

"Yippee, that's a great idea," Carrie squealed. She got up and danced around the table. Sarah jumped up and followed her, both clapping their hands.

Jan laughed. "Ok, girls, sit and finish your supper."

Sarah skidded back to her chair and looked up at Jan. She grabbed her cup of milk. "That sounds like fun, Mom. What's a butterfly garden?"

Ben chuckled. "Well, Sarah, it's a flower garden that attracts butterflies."

Carrie took a big bite of noodles and wiped her mouth with her hand. "Yeah, Sarah, we can plant lots of flowers and the butterflies will come and eat them. My teacher called it *pollen*. Is that right, Mom?"

Jan got up and retrieved the pitcher of iced tea, filling her glass. She lifted it up to Ben. At his nod, she refilled his, too. "Well, that's sort of right, Carrie," she said, setting the pitcher on the table and sitting down. "You plant a certain type of flower which attracts butterflies, then the butterflies drink the nectar from the flowers." She chuckled. "It's sort of like Kool-Aid for butterflies." She stared at her family. "You know, the more I think about it, the better I like this idea. We have memorial money in Wanda's name." She glanced at Carrie. "And I bet your class would love to help."

After everyone finished eating, Jan got up again and started cleaning off the table. "I'll talk to the trustees and figure out the best place to put the garden. We can get a plaque with Wanda's name on it and place it amidst the flowers."

"Sounds great," Ben said, getting to his feet. "Here, I'll do the dishes. Why don't you get the girls ready for bed?"

Jan followed the girls into the bathroom to prepare for their baths. Excitement flowed through her as plans formed in her head. The garden could be planted in early March. She could get mature plants so they should be blooming by Easter, which was in mid-April. And she was certain she could find butterflies somewhere and release them at the end of the Easter service. Jan smiled as she ran the bath water. Light and hope chased away some of the darkness that had plagued her heart since Wanda's death. God was showing her a way to turn this horrible tragedy into something beautiful.

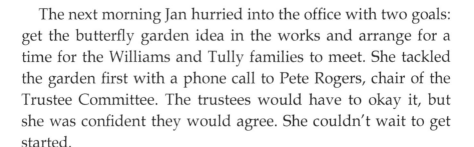

The next morning Jan hurried into the office with two goals: get the butterfly garden idea in the works and arrange for a time for the Williams and Tully families to meet. She tackled the garden first with a phone call to Pete Rogers, chair of the Trustee Committee. The trustees would have to okay it, but she was confident they would agree. She couldn't wait to get started.

"Hi Pete, this is Pastor Jan," she said when Pete answered. "I have an idea how to use the money given in memory of Wanda. We could plant a butterfly garden and put a plaque with Wanda's name in it. I hope to get the children from Wanda's class to help. We could dedicate the garden at the Easter service and perhaps release butterflies." Jan was so excited about the project that she didn't notice Pete had not responded. She finally stopped and realized that all she heard was silence.

"Pete, are you there?"

Oh, no, something's wrong.

"Pete?"

After a few moments, Pete finally spoke. "Ah, Pastor Jan, the trustees have already decided to use that money toward roof repairs."

Jan's pulse jumped. Pete continued to speak about how they had gotten together right after the funeral and made plans to use the several hundred dollars. Jan's face flamed. As the pastor, she needed to be included in this decision. *Can't believe they didn't talk to me about this.* She started to interrupt him and tell him designated memorial money couldn't be used for church repairs but caught herself and tried to calm down. Wanda's death and the fire had sapped her strength. She didn't want to fight the trustees. *Take a deep breath, Jan, and listen. Then speak.*

"Pete," she finally interrupted him, "I appreciate the trustees acting on this so quickly, but the memorial money should be used in a way that honors Wanda. I really don't think roof repairs will do that." Jan was trying hard not to get defensive. If there was one thing she had learned in the last few months, it was she needed to stay calm and explain her decisions.

"Oh, sorry, Pastor Jan, we thought you were so busy looking after the Williams family and taking care of the church folks that we would just go ahead and take care of this. We were all together after the funeral anyhow and just decided to take a straw vote."

All together my foot. Here they are doing things without me again. But again, Jan took a deep breath. Perhaps Pete and the trustees were only trying to help. "Well, how about calling a meeting for next week and let's talk about this?"

"Sure, Pastor Jan. We'll have it next Tuesday night. I'll give everyone a call. Sorry, we just wanted to help you out."

"I know, Pete. Thanks." She hung up and sighed. She had been in Baylorsville for almost nine months, but the trustees still didn't see fit to include her in major decisions affecting the church property. She stood and walked to the window, watching the oak leaves gently blowing in the light wind. Though she was frustrated with the trustees, she was grateful Pete had listened to her and was pleased he had agreed to call the trustees together to hear her plan about the use of the memorial money. Maybe she was finally gaining some authority. She thought about the conversation with the Tullys. They had trusted her enough to share their very private and painful story. And Pete had accepted her idea. Yes, it had been a difficult week, filled with emotions about Wanda's death and the aftermath of the fire. But through these horrific events, it looked like the congregation was beginning to give her the authority as pastor. She smiled and walked back to her desk.

Chapter Twenty-Five

After lunch that afternoon, Jan decided to visit with the Williams family to talk through the proposed butterfly project rather than simply phone them. She hoped the garden would be an avenue to heal both the Williamses and the church, and she wanted to make sure Linda and Tom were on board.

Linda and Tom were on the front porch, holding hands and rocking on the swing when Jan arrived. Sadness pierced her heart. *God, help them through this.* After hugs, Jan sat on an old, rustic gray rocking chair, and Tom left to get her a glass of iced tea.

"It was a wonderful service, Pastor Jan. Thanks so much for all you did for us," Linda said. She looked up as Tom came back with three glasses, handed one to Jan and sat on the porch swing next to his wife. Linda took the other glasses, set them on the table, and grabbed his hand.

"God was certainly speaking through all of it," Jan said.

"Yeah, Pastor Jan, thanks," Tom said. "Sorry I've been so moody. It's like I'm living in a fog."

"No need to apologize, Tom. It'll seem unreal for a long time. You don't get over the death of a child, you just learn how to live with it."

"Don't figure I'll ever learn to live with it. I just miss Wanda so much." Tom started crying, wiping his eyes with his hands.

Jan touched his hand as Linda, sniffling herself, embraced her husband. Jan waited as Tom hiccupped and grabbed some tissue, which was lying on the table. He blew his nose and took a deep breath.

"I'm sorry, Pastor Jan, I don't always blubber like this. It's… it's just that I've felt I've had to hold it together for the family and," he looked at Linda, "my wife here."

Linda smiled and took more tissues to wipe his eyes. It was a touching gesture and brought tears to Jan's eyes. *God, please help me find a way to help them.* Linda hugged Tom again.

"It's okay, Tom. I can't imagine what you and Linda are going through. What I do know is that God is with you."

Tom took a large gulp of tea. "It's so hard," he sighed, looking down and shaking his head, "but we need to move on for Mary's sake."

"By the way, how is Mary?" Jan asked.

Linda reached across and placed her hand on Tom's shoulder. "Mary is still confused. Sometimes she forgets and asks where Wanda is." She looked back at Jan. "She put the pink rose from the service on Wanda's bed."

Jan smiled. "Maybe that's her way of staying close to Wanda." Jan sat back in her chair. "Speaking of moving on, I've got something I want to talk with you about that might really help Mary. There's been some money donated to the church in memory of Wanda. Carrie said the children in her class were talking about butterfly gardens and I wondered if the church could create a butterfly garden in memory of Wanda." Jan studied their reaction. Linda's eyes got wide and filled with tears. She clutched Tom's hand, as tears formed in his eyes again.

Jan's heart started racing. She didn't want to upset them. Something was obviously causing them both great anxiety, but her fear was relieved when Linda leaned toward Jan and grabbed her hand, too.

"Oh, Pastor Jan, this is so amazing," Linda said. "I know this sounds odd, but a few days before Wanda," her voice cracked,

"… died, she sat up in bed and started talking about this big yellow butterfly flying in her room. I thought she had dreamed it, but do you think she really saw one?"

Wow, God, what amazing grace. A shiver went down Jan's spine. "Yeah, Linda, I think Wanda did see a butterfly, one God sent just for her." Jan's voice broke as she tried to compose herself. "So, I guess this means you like the idea."

Linda got up to hug Jan. "Yes, Pastor Jan, a butterfly garden would be a wonderful way to remember her." She looked at Tom as he, too, nodded.

"Great, I'll put that into motion right away. We could plant it early in March and invite the children of Wanda's class to help. Then we could dedicate it Easter Sunday."

"Oh, that sounds wonderful," Linda said. "And I'm sure Mary would really like to help. Thank you so much."

Jan stood up. "Well, that's settled then. I'd better be going. I'll get you the details later. Before I leave, can we have prayer?"

After praying, Jan left to pick up the girls from school. As she drove, her heart warmed as a deep awareness of God's presence filled her. It had been an awful week with the fire and Wanda's death, but God was taking the brokenness of this town and beginning to create healing. And Jan was grateful she had played a small part. She smiled.

Chapter Twenty-Six

The idea of the butterfly garden was a tremendous hit with Carrie's teacher. After the trustees put their stamp of approval on it, she and the leaders of the church set aside the first Saturday in March to plant the garden. The flowers would have time to bloom to attract the butterflies before Easter, which was late this year, in mid-April.

The day of the planting dawned bright and clear. The girls skipped in front of Jan as they headed to the church that morning. Ben would come later in the car with a collection of rakes, shovels, and spades. Fluffy clouds, like balls of cotton, dotted the deep blue sky. A cool breeze stirred the old, dead leaves and swept many of them off the street in front of the church. Jan had high hopes the community would show up today to help create this garden. This would be an important event to show how Jan's leadership was affecting this community.

When Jan got to the courtyard of the church, with Carrie and Sarah running before her, John Tully's truck was already backed into the yard. His truck bed was full of the rich black dirt that would provide the basis for the garden. Martha was helping Betty set up cups and napkins for the lemonade and iced tea. Pete was pulling up his truck, which held the pine straw mulch for the garden, alongside John's. Another trustee had gone to Tallahassee the day before to buy the thirty plants. The decision was made to buy plants already blooming, so there was a colorful array of white Wild Indigo, purple Verbena and orange and yellow Lantana plants lining the sidewalk under the awning of the adult Sunday school wing. As more people arrived, Jan stood and breathed in the scene. *God, let this morning be healing for us as we dig in this dirt and plant these flowers.*

A squeal from Sarah alerted Jan to the Williams' car pulling into the parking lot. Sarah hugged Mary as she got out of the car while Jan greeted Tom and Linda.

"Oh, Pastor Jan, look how many people have come," Linda said, glancing around the crowd. Several more cars had now pulled up. Jan noticed Carrie's teacher with five or six children already gathered around her.

"Yes, Linda, it's so good to see everyone." She gave Linda a hug. "Today's going to be a great day. Would you like to help with the cookies?"

She gestured toward Betty and walked Linda over to the table where the goodies were. Out of the corner of her eye, she noticed Tom heading toward the trucks. John stopped shoveling long enough to shake Tom's hand. Jan smiled. She had decided not to talk to Tom and Linda about getting with the Tullys. She hoped that Martha and John would initiate that instead. It looked like it was happening as John pulled Tom aside and began a hushed conversation. *Thank you, God.*

After Ben showed up with more shovels, he and the men finished preparing the garden for the plants. By this time, a dozen children from both the church and Wanda's class, along with their parents, were milling around, looking at the plants, munching on cookies, and chatting. At a nod from John, Jan called out to everyone.

"Friends, we're making this butterfly garden today to honor and remember our sweet Wanda, who loved butterflies and flowers." Jan looked over at Linda and Tom, who were holding hands. They both smiled at her. "When we think about Wanda, we can come to this garden and remember how special she was to us." Jan smiled as she remembered the yellow butterfly Wanda had seen right before she died. *This garden will be special to me, too.*

She walked over to the plants and called to the children. "Okay, kids, come here." She pointed to the first line of flowers. "This plant is a Lantana. Isn't it pretty?" At several *oohs* and *aahs* from the group, Jan continued. "When this plant and the others," she gestured to the rows before her, "are planted in our garden, butterflies will come."

"And eat the nectar," Carrie interrupted, beaming.

As several other children shouted out "yeah, that's right" and clapped, Jan laughed.

"Thanks, Carrie, glad you were paying attention in class." Jan looked over to her teacher, who smiled. "So, when we plant this garden, butterflies will come here to eat. Not only will the church have beautiful colorful plants, but we can also enjoy the beauty of the butterflies. So, I'm going to give each of you a plant. You see the holes that our men have dug. You're just going to tuck them in like you were tucking them into bed." Jan demonstrated by placing one of the purple Verbenas in the first hole.

The trustees, along with the third-grade teacher, had decided to let the children put the plants in the ground. They would get dirty, which was part of the fun, and someone would have to come behind them to make sure the plants were in the ground right, but this would give ownership of the garden to Wanda's class. Later, these children would get to water and weed the garden, too. The plaque with Wanda's picture on it at the front of the garden would remind the children of her.

"Now, let's pray over these plants." Jan gathered them in a circle, held hands, and prayed, "Jesus, these are your plants. Help them grow into beautiful flowers so the butterflies will come. And help us remember sweet Wanda every time we see both the flowers and the butterflies. Amen."

"I'm going to give Mary the first plant." Jan handed Mary an orange Lantana. Tom and Linda helped her plant it. Everyone clapped, and the children lined up to get their plants. Jan observed the happy, chaotic scene. *God, this is your amazing grace.* Her heart warmed when John knelt beside Sarah and helped her push dirt around her plant. Through God's help, Jan was making a difference in this small town.

Amidst the laughing children and chattering adults, Ben came up to Jan. He put his arm around her and said, "Looks like a huge success."

"Yeah, this is a great day." Jan put her arm around Ben's waist. Yes, it was an incredible scene. The church, her church, was on the way to healing. And Jan felt a new confidence in herself and her role as the pastor. *Thank you, God, for this holy time.*

Chapter *Twenty-Seven*

Easter arrived amidst chirping birds and the promise of a warm day. Jan walked to the church early to check on the service preparations. In the butterfly garden, pink, yellow, white, and purple flowers bloomed and sparkled in the dew. The fresh, brown pine straw mulch, which had been carefully spread around the new plants, gave a stark contrast to the colors of the flowers. Jan ran her hand over the bronze plaque placed in the ground at the front of the garden. She read aloud the words etched there. "In memory of Wanda Jean Williams–God's Sweet Angel". Tears formed in Jan's eyes, which she quickly brushed away. *No time for tears now.*

She turned from the garden and entered the church by the front stone steps. It was an hour before anyone would be in the church, so she had the place to herself. The sweet smell of the white lilies, which decorated the altar, hung in the air. Her gaze swept across the sanctuary as she relived the last several months: her first service, her first funeral, the countless sermons, the many visits, the fire, Wanda's death. But this would be her first Easter and, like the Christmas Eve service, it was a pivotal time for her. And yet, she discovered, to her amazement, the worship service didn't concern her on this Easter morning. Rather, she joyfully anticipated God's amazing presence. She sat in the front pew of the empty church. *I am the pastor here.*

And I truly love these people, my people.

Startled, a thought crossed her mind. She had called them "my" people. And to her surprise she realized they *were* her people. She had grown to love them, even the difficult ones. She smiled. *Thanks God. Be with me today. Speak through me.*

Jan's heart swelled as she followed the choir, singing "Christ the Lord Has Risen Today" through the packed church. The ushers were busy putting chairs in the outer aisles to accommodate the latecomers. During the last verse of the hymn, as she stood behind the pulpit, her eyes scanned the crowd. John and Martha Tully sat with the Williams family with little Mary tucked in between John and Tom. *Thanks for that miracle, God.*

She locked eyes with Ben, who sat in the front pew. Carrie and Sarah, in their matching pink Easter dresses with white stockings and patent leather shoes, nestled on either side of him. Carrie was growing up. It had been a struggle to get her to wear the same dress as her sister. Jan almost laughed remembering how indignant Carrie was. "Mom, we're not twins!" *Bet this is the last year we'll get away with that.*

After the congregation finished the opening hymn, Jan raised her hands and proclaimed, "Christ the Lord is risen!" The people responded with, "He is risen indeed." Her first Easter with these people, *her people*, had begun.

Joyful singing filled the church. The choir sang a compelling rendition of "Up from the Grave, He Arose" and Jan knew her sermon sharing God's joyous ending of the empty tomb touched the congregation. But it was the conclusion of the service that excited her the most.

Right before the final hymn, she called the children of the congregation to come up front. She announced she had a special surprise for them. Carrie and Sarah squirmed in their seats. They knew about Jan's plan and before Jan could finish, they bounded out of the pew and headed up to the altar rail. A few children got up and followed, but others had to be coaxed by their parents. Going forward for a special children's moment was new to them.

She sat the children on the cushions of the altar rail. They were a rainbow of colors with their new dresses and pastel shirts and ties. Amidst giggles and elbowing, they finally settled down. Jan sat with them, with Sarah snuggled on her lap.

"Hi, my friends. I want to tell you a special story this Easter morning. It's about a caterpillar named Julia and a grasshopper named Bernie. They were great friends and played together. Bernie hopped around and Julia happily crawled after him. They had lots of fun until the days started turning colder." Jan had the children's attention. Every eye was on her.

She continued. "Then Julia grew tired and her body began to change. She couldn't keep up with Bernie, who continued to hop around, and she was sad, and afraid. She wanted to crawl into a bush and hide."

Carrie's hand shot up and before Jan could shush her, she blurted out, "I know what's happening. Julia is turning into a.... what's it called?" Carrie scrunched up her face. "Oh, I know, Julia is turning into a chrysalis."

"Well, that's very true, Carrie," Jan said as several people in the congregation laughed. "Julia was turning into a chrysalis, but she didn't understand what that meant and she was frightened."

Some of the children reacted with sighs and "oh no's," and Jan smiled at them. She continued. "But her friend, Bernie, who was older and wiser and had seen this type of thing before, told her that it was okay. As Carrie said, Julia was preparing to turn into a butterfly." Carrie beamed and her head nodded.

Jan watched the children's eyes grow wide. They were hanging onto every word. Sarah snuggled closer to her as Jan continued. "But Julia was worried. She had never been a butterfly before. What would she look like? Would she feel different? Would anyone recognize her? The days got colder and Julia gradually stopped her daily walks with Bernie. She hung upside down under a bush and became very still."

"Oh, no," little Mary Williams cried out.

Sarah crawled out of Jan's lap and squatted beside Mary, patting her on the head. "It's okay, Mary."

Jan's heart warmed as murmurs spread throughout the church. This story was really touching people.

"Julia remained still for a very long time. But suddenly, she woke up, and, guess what? She had changed again."

Six-year-old Joey, one of the Rollins boys, thrust his hand in the air and, before Jan could call on him, yelled, "Julia became a butterfly, just like Carrie said."

Several in the congregation laughed and Carrie started clapping as Joey joined in. Jan stifled her own laugh. She needed to finish the story before the children finished it for her.

 She placed her hand on Carrie to quiet her and said, "Yes, Joey, that's exactly what happened, and Julia was no longer afraid. The darkness had disappeared into bright sunlight. Julia was different. She tried crawling and instead…" Jan paused and locked eyes with a few of the children. "What do you think she did?"

"She flew!" several of them yelled out.

Jan laughed, along with many in the congregation. "That's right, she flew. And she was beautiful. She loved the yellow and orange of her wings as she soared over the trees. Seeing Bernie, who was hopping around, looking very excited, Julia cried out, 'Look at me, Bernie, I'm a butterfly now. I'm free from the darkness, and I feel wonderful.'"

Jan smiled at the children, who were jumping and laughing. She also looked out at the congregation and saw several smiling. Standing, she said, "Friends, it's Easter morning. The tomb is empty. Jesus has risen from the dead. We, like Julia, can shout and proclaim, 'I'm not afraid anymore. I'm free of the dark, and it feels wonderful.'"

Several "amens" erupted from the congregation.

"Now, boys and girls, I have another surprise," she said, trying to calm the children. "Everyone sit back down." She nodded to Ben, who stepped to a side door that led to a storage room. Both Sarah and Carrie gave Jan a questioning look. Jan grinned. *You girls didn't know about this.*

Ben came out of the room holding a small plastic cage. Bits of grass were in the bottom and a screen was on top. He carried it to Jan, and she knelt so the children could see.

"It's butterflies!" several shouted.

"Yes, it's butterflies from Mrs. Hobbs' class." She glanced at Carrie who was beaming and nodding. "These butterflies started as caterpillars, then became chrysalises, and finally turned into butterflies."

"Just like … what's her name?… Julia!" shouted Sarah as Mary echoed it, and both of them jumped up and started twirling around the other children.

Jan laughed along with most of the congregation as the children gathered around the container. "Yes, just like Julia."

Jan rose and raised the cage over her head. "To end our Easter service the children and I are going to go outside to the new butterfly garden and release these butterflies."

Several of the children shouted and a few, including Sarah and Carrie started dancing. Jan smiled at them. "Hold on guys, let me finish." Jan continued her instructions to the congregation. "The choir will follow us, leading us in our final song. This is a new song. I first heard it at a women's retreat I attended last year. It will be included in our new *United Methodist Hymnal*, which will come out soon, and I hope you love it as much as I do. The words are printed in your bulletins, and the choir will lead you."

She looked at the excited children and said, "So guys, let's get going." She led the children through the church as the choir followed them.

Jan and the children gathered around the butterfly garden. The congregation gathered around them. Accompanied by the organ heard through the open church windows, the choir led them in singing "The Hymn of Promise."

In the bulb there is a flower, in the sea, an apple tree,
in cocoons, a hidden promise, butterflies will soon be free!
In the cold and snow of winter there's a spring that waits to be,
Unrevealed until its season, something God alone can see.
There's a song in every silence, seeking word and melody,
There's a dawn in every darkness, bringing hope to you and me.
From the past will come the future, what it holds, a mystery,
Unrevealed until its season, something God alone can see.

As the congregation sang, Jan gazed at her people. The children had calmed as if knowing this was a holy moment. Tom and Linda, with Mary between them, were standing over Wanda's memorial plaque. John and Martha stood beside them, holding their hands. Betty Smith, as usual, was crying. People were still filing out of the church as they sang the final verse:

In our end is our beginning, in our time, infinity;
in our doubt there is believing, in our life, eternity.
In our death, a resurrection, at the last, a victory,
Unrevealed until its season, something God alone can see.

Jan lifted the small cage in the air as Ben reached over and unfastened the screen. The three butterflies flew out as Jan said, "We end our Easter service this morning claiming the resurrection of Jesus. We also remember little Wanda, who would have loved watching these butterflies. In the last moments of her life…" Jan swallowed hard and glanced at Tom and Linda, who were crying yet smiling. Jan gained her composure and continued, "In the last moments of Wanda's life she looked up at her mother and said, 'Mom, do you see that big yellow butterfly? Isn't it pretty?'"

Jan stopped for a moment as sobs and "amens" echoed

throughout the crowd. She then turned around to face the garden and, with arms raised in the traditional benediction, said, "We dedicate this garden in memory of Wanda Jean Williams, but we give our lives to you this morning, O God, in sure and certain hope in the resurrection of Jesus Christ. Amen and amen."

The organist, who had been leaning out an open window waiting for the benediction, blasted out the postlude as the people began to disperse. It was not an ordinary ending of an Easter service, but it was one they would never forget. Many of the congregation milled about, looking at the garden, hugging Tom and Linda, and chatting with each other. Ben came up to Jan and kissed her lightly on the cheek.

"Good job, Jan."

"Thanks." They held hands and watched the children chase butterflies. Jan reflected on the last nine months. The difficulties with John and the pastoral work she had done with Wanda's death and the fire had certainly been hard but had also endeared her to this church and community. She thought back to the jitters she had on that first Sunday and smiled. She had not only survived these months, but she had also thrived in this ministry. She had truly become the Pastor of First Church.

CPSIA information can be obtained
at www.ICGtesting.com
Printed in the USA
BVHW081741070720
583082BV00008B/15